Also by Michaela MacColl

Always Emily

Nobody's Secret

Promise the Night

Prisoners in the Palace

The *Revelation* *of* **LOUISA MAY**

A NOVEL OF INTRIGUE AND ROMANCE BY

MICHAELA MacCOLL

CHRONICLE BOOKS

SAN FRANCISCO

All quotations are from *Little Women* by Louisa May Alcott.

Library of Congress Cataloging-in-Publication Data:

MacColl, Michaela, author.

The revelation of Louisa May : a novel of intrigue and romance / by Michaela MacColl.

pages cm

Summary: Louisa May Alcott has problems–her mother is taking a job over a hundred miles
away to earn some money, leaving to it to Louisa to care for the family, her father refuses to
work for money, a fugitive slave is seeking refuge in their house, and a slave catcher has been
murdered, making the Underground Railroad much more dangerous.

ISBN 978-1-4521-3357-7 (alk. paper)

1. Alcott, Louisa May, 1832-1888–Juvenile fiction. 2. Underground Railroad–Massachu-
setts--Juvenile fiction. 3. Fugitive slaves–United States–History–19th century–Juvenile
fiction. 4. Families–Massachusetts–Concord–Juvenile fiction. 5. Murder–Massachusetts–
Concord–Juvenile fiction. 6. Concord (Mass.)–History–19th century–Juvenile fiction. [1.
Alcott, Louisa May, 1832-1888–Fiction. 2. Underground Railroad–Fiction. 3. Fugitive
slaves–Fiction. 4. Slavery–Fiction. 5. Family life–Massachusetts–Concord–Fiction. 6.
Murder–Fiction. 7. Concord (Mass.)–History–19th century–Fiction.] I. Title.

PZ7.M13384Re 2015
813.6--dc23
2014028073

Manufactured in China.

Design by Sara Schneider.
Typeset in Hoefler Text, Copperplate, and Shelley Allegro.

10 9 8 7 6 5 4 3 2 1

Chronicle Books LLC
680 Second Street
San Francisco, CA 94107

Chronicle Books—we see things differently. Become part of our community at
www.chroniclebooks.com/teen.

In memory of my dear friend,
Catherine Topp Amon
(1957 – 2014)

CHAPTER ONE

"Don't you wish we had the money papa
lost when we were little, Jo?
Dear me! How happy and good we'd be,
if we had no worries!"

$\mathcal{Y}$ou're leaving me?"

Her father's words floated through the cracks in the door.

Louisa stifled a cry. Marmee would never leave them. Through all their suffering, the one constant was that the family must and would stay together.

Abandoning her desk, Louisa pressed her ear to the door that led to the parlor. She strained to hear her mother's answer.

"Bronson, you've left me no choice." Marmee's voice was tight, as though her vocal cords had been wrung like a wet rag.

Louisa opened the door with one finger, just a bit, to see her mother pacing back and forth across the narrow parlor. With a ripple of shock, Louisa noticed that Marmee's dark gray-streaked hair had come loose from her bun. Louisa stroked one of her own untidy braids in solidarity.

"I can't economize any more," Marmee said. "We've used up our credit in every shop in Concord. We can't afford to stay in this house or buy necessaries for the children." Her voice grew stronger, then faded as she paced away from the door. "If you won't work for money, I shall have to. It's a good job. They want me to run the hotel and manage the water cures."

Craning her neck, Louisa could just make out her father's face, as handsome and stubborn as ever. But his voice shook as he said, "It's so far. Waterford is a hundred and fifty miles away. What if the children need you?" Father was reclining on the comfortable sofa, his hands interlaced behind his gray-streaked blond head, his long legs stretched out in front of him. But his indifference was a pose; he would be lost without Marmee. They all would be.

"What the children need is to go to school," Marmee said. "But we can't afford it."

"Bah! What better teachers could they have besides me, Emerson, and Thoreau?" he asked with his usual confidence.

"Millionaires would pay a fortune for their children to have such an education."

"But their education, such as it is, lacks method and discipline."

"All the better!" Bronson exclaimed. "You know my methods. Our children thrive without the confines of a schoolroom and a harsh schoolmaster."

"Anna is only seventeen and she has to work for her living far from home. And what about Louisa? She should be going to parties and enjoying herself, as I did when I was her age." Poor Marmee—her voice was so tired and discouraged.

"When I was their age I was working on the farm," Bronson argued.

"But I enjoyed Boston's finest society, going to the theater and to parties. I want the girls to have some fun in their lives."

Huddled against the door, Louisa slid down to the floor and sighed. She definitely would prefer the theater to working for a living. Louisa knew she should find a job like Anna had, but she hated teaching and sewing and all the respectable ways she could earn money. And anything that pulled her away from writing her stories and poems was a waste of her time.

"A little sacrifice is good for them," Bronson said. "Our daughters must seek fields of richer thyme than we grow here. Let each of them make honey for herself, since all lasting enjoyments come from one's own exertions." Louisa heard him get up and rummage about the small desk in the parlor.

Louisa pushed open the door a little further. Her father was writing in one of his leather-bound journals. "That bit about bees is quite good," he muttered. "I might work that into one of my Conversations."

Marmee stood, her profile to Louisa, watching him write. The line of her back was rigid, and her hands were clenched. "You haven't had a paying Conversation in months, Bronson," Marmee said hotly. Then with a deliberate calming breath, Marmee moved close to her husband and placed her work-worn hands on his shoulders. "Come with me!" she murmured in his ear. "The hotel would like you to come and teach classes. They think you would be a great attraction." Her voice became husky. "You'd be supporting the family, and we could be together."

"Ah," breathed Louisa. So this was Marmee's plan.

Her parents had moved to a part of the room where she couldn't see them. Just as she moved to nudge the door open, she heard footsteps, light but firm, crossing the floor. She pulled back. The door closed with a decisive click.

She pressed her ear against the door, straining to hear her father's response to Marmee's entreaty.

"My dear, my work is in my mind and in the hard labor I do to grow our food and fix our house." Father's voice was only slightly muffled by the oak door. "I have no calling to work for others. Do not ask me to compromise my principles for money!"

"You would have us starve for your principles instead?" Even without seeing them, Louisa could tell her mother was close to tears.

Her father's voice took on a wheedling sound that put Louisa's teeth on edge. "Abba, you used to be proud of my ideas and principles. But you've changed, grown cold and unsympathetic. Now you complain like the most common housewife that there isn't enough money for fripperies."

Louisa glanced up at the few dresses hanging in her narrow closet. Each one was a hand-me-down from some rich relation, turned out and resewn to make a serviceable gown. Fripperies? She'd gladly settle for a fresh bolt of calico.

"Fripperies? Bronson, there isn't any money to pay for firewood. Or flour. Or your precious journals."

"Your family . . ."

"My family's generosity has been exhausted time and time again. Even my brother, who admires you greatly, wonders why you will gladly take the money that others have worked for, but you won't work yourself."

Louisa had only the vaguest memories of her father ever working for his living. When she was three, he had a school in Boston. His revolutionary ideas included fresh air in the classroom, no corporal punishment, and the strange idea that children could also teach the teachers. At first wealthy parents had flocked to the school, but Bronson's other ideas about religion had frightened them away. When Bronson admitted a black girl as a pupil, he lost his final backers. Almost sixteen now, Louisa couldn't recall her father working for money any time since, no matter how bare the larder. Father's willingness to let the family suffer for his ideals had been proven beyond a scintilla of doubt.

Marmee went on, ice in her voice. "I've been offered a contract for three months and you give me no choice but to take it."

Bronson sank into an armchair and wiped his brow. "But who will take care of me?"

Louisa pressed her forehead against the doorjamb, steeling herself against the answer.

"Louisa will," Marmee said. "She's a fine housekeeper."

Louisa scrambled to her feet and burst into the room. "Marmee! You can't leave me here to do everything! Beth's no help—she's still recovering from her winter cold. And baby May won't do anything but draw. You expect me to do all the cooking and the cleaning and the shopping and take care of them, too? I'll never have the chance to write." She was running out of breath, so she made sure to finish with a flourish. "It's not fair that just because Father won't get a job I have to be a slave!"

"Louisa!" both Marmee and Bronson cried at once.

"A young lady never stoops to eavesdropping," Marmee said in a forbidding voice.

"Honest labor to care for your family is not slavery!" Bronson scolded as his wife took a breath. "You've met true slaves. You know the cruelty they suffer. By comparing your-self to a slave, you demean both you and them."

Louisa closed her eyes and pressed her fists against her eyelids. "I'm sorry," she whispered.

"Go back to your room," Marmee said. "And quietly. There's no need to wake your sisters. We'll talk later."

Her eyes averted from her parents, Louisa slowly crossed the parlor to her room, closing her door behind her. When they had bought Hillside House a few years ago, the house had been too small for Father, Mother, and four Alcott daughters, not to mention all the constant visitors. So her inventive father had cut an old workshop on the property in two and grafted each half onto opposite sides of the house. Louisa's tiny room, the first she had ever had to call her own, was in one half of the repurposed building, with a second door that opened directly into the garden.

Louisa shoved her bare feet into her boots, jerked her shawl from its hook, and slipped into the garden. Her ability to sneak out at night was her private antidote to the press of so many people. The chilled night air stung her skin and a breeze stirred her nightdress about her knees. Perched on a bench her father had fashioned from an old log, she brought her knees up to her chin.

Marmee couldn't leave them. Father could and did, travel-ing often to talk to other philosophers. But Marmee was their rock. Their shield against poverty and despair. Their financial situation must be even worse than Louisa knew for Marmee to consider leaving. But Louisa had only been thinking of how it affected her. She was ashamed of her own selfishness.

Money. Money. Money. How she hated being dependent on the kindness of friends and family. Louisa was tired of being grateful. She had looked for a job in Concord but there were none to be had. It was a pretty place, but dull. The townspeople thought the Alcotts were wild and strange. It was only because of Mr. Emerson that they had moved there. If it weren't for him and Mr. Thoreau, Concord would indeed be the "cold, heartless, brainless, soulless Concord" Marmee called it. But even Mr. Emerson couldn't conjure up work so Louisa could contribute to the family's finances.

The house faced busy Lexington Road, although it was mostly quiet at this hour. From the corner of her eye, Louisa caught a glimpse of movement in the shrubs by the front windows. She retreated to her door and reached for the stout walking stick she kept there.

"Who's there?" she called, forcing a quaver down.

A cracking noise of a foot on a twig, then a deliberate silence.

"I said, who is there?" Holding the walking stick up in front of her face, she stepped forward and peered around the corner. Next to the parlor's big bay window there was a dark figure, barely visible against the olive color of the house. Suddenly, the figure blinked, revealing the frightened whites of his eyes. She realized that his darkness was not the cover of night but the color of his skin.

"What's your business here?" she asked, her voice stern.

"Excuse me, Miss." The man's voice was deep and hesitant. "Are you the Stationmaster?"

Louisa sighed. Exactly what the Alcott family needed right now. Another fugitive slave.

CHAPTER TWO

There were not in all the city four merrier people
than the hungry little girls
who gave away their breakfasts and contented
themselves with bread and milk . . .

*L*ouisa put her finger to her lips and motioned for the man to follow her inside through her bedroom to the parlor.

Bronson and Marmee were sitting apart from each other on the sofa. They looked up, startled, when Louisa appeared in the doorway.

"Louy, I told you to wait for me," Marmee said.

"Until you learn to curb your impatience," Bronson said, "you will never discipline your mind."

Louisa sighed and stepped to one side so they could see the fugitive standing behind her.

The man was big, boasting more inches than even Bronson, who had to duck going through the doors of his own home. The original parts of the house dated back over a century, when people built low ceilings to keep in heat. It was a sore trial to the Alcotts, who tended to grow tall.

Standing in the center of the parlor, hunched slightly, the fugitive kept his hands close to his thighs as though he was loath to touch the furniture or the whitewashed walls. A battered canvas knapsack hung over his shoulder.

Irritations and quarrels forgotten, Marmee flew from her seat and closed the curtains. Although most of their friends and neighbors hated slavery as much as the Alcotts did, one never knew who might be tempted by a reward for information about an escaped slave. And it wasn't only the slave who was at risk; the Alcotts could be prosecuted for sheltering him.

Bronson stood and held his hands out wide. "My name is Bronson Alcott. You are welcome and safe in my home."

The fugitive stared for the briefest moment, then smiled broadly. "God bless you, sir."

"What is your name?" Bronson asked.

"My name is George Simmons. But Simmons was my owner's name, and my first Conductor warned me that they'll look for me under that name. So lately I've been thinking my name is George Freedman."

"A noble name," Bronson said, approval warming his voice. "Where have you come from?"

"I came from Virginia. I've been running for two weeks."

"And where is your Conductor?" Marmee asked. "Why are you traveling alone? We had no message that we would be receiving a package tonight."

"I stayed in Dedham last night. My Conductor had an illness in his house, so he sent me to Concord without him. He said I could count on the folks in the house set up against the hill on the Lexington Road."

"Dedham is nearly twenty-five miles from here!" Marmee exclaimed. "You must be exhausted."

"Ma'am, I feel as if I've been running forever."

Outside a carriage rattled past, its lantern briefly illuminating the road. George froze and his eyes scanned the room as if searching for a hiding place. Louisa took pity and stepped to the window. Staying hidden behind the curtain, she parted the chintz drapes just wide enough to watch the stagecoach disappear down the Lexington Road.

"It's all right. They have passed us by," she said, filling her voice with reassurance. She had found George; he was her responsibility. Glancing over at the fugitive she recognized the look in his eyes. Hunger. "Marmee, shouldn't we get George something to eat?"

"Of course," Marmee said firmly. "You must be starving."

"Yes, ma'am. The last time I ate was yesterday morning."

"Louisa, warm up the leftover soup and feed George a proper meal."

Louisa didn't need telling twice. She turned on her heel, knocking a book off the bookcase in her haste. Once in the kitchen, she poked at the kitchen coals to coax a flame. She opened up the icebox and pulled out the pot with the leftover soup from dinner. If George hoped for meat, he would be disappointed. Bronson Alcott permitted no living creatures to be sacrificed for the family's dinner. But they had plenty of vegetables from their own garden and enough potato to thicken the broth and fill an empty stomach.

Bronson led George into the kitchen, where he sluiced water over his face, removing the sweat of fear and the dirt of his time on the road. Not many homes had a water pump inside; it was one of the many improvements Bronson had made to the house.

"I'm obliged, Mr. Alcott," he said.

"Call me Bronson. Sit down here at the table."

Marmee brought a plate with bread and placed it in front of George. He hesitated and she put a slice in his hand, ordering him with a gentle smile, "Eat."

"Are you traveling alone?" Bronson said.

"The others are a few days behind me."

"Others?" Louisa asked, bringing their guest a mug of cold water. She hoped there weren't too many; the Alcotts couldn't afford to feed them.

"My wife and children are traveling separately," George said, and his expressive eyes turned mournful.

"How could you divide your family?" Bronson asked with a meaningful glance at his wife.

"I'm sure George was doing what was best for them," Marmee retorted.

"How tragic to leave your children behind," Louisa said, for once united with her father against Marmee. "Aren't you worried about them?"

"A parent does whatever is required to keep them from harm," Marmee answered.

With a puzzled look distributed evenly among all the Alcotts, George explained, "My Conductor said they'd travel safer without me. I'm the one the catcher's looking for. I was useful to my master because I can read, write, and do figures. He posted a large reward."

"Barbaric," murmured Bronson.

Louisa shivered despite the heat of the stove. She had seen those "Wanted: Fugitive Slave" posters in Boston. They were put up sometimes in Concord, too, but Louisa and her sisters would pull them down. Even her vivid imagination couldn't envision being hunted like an animal. "The catcher?" she asked.

George hesitated, wringing his hands. "I heard from the last Conductor that a catcher is on my trail. He's a Northerner and a big man. That's all I know." His eyes darted around the snug kitchen. "I don't want to bring trouble here."

Louisa glanced at her parents' determined faces. Even the threat of arrest wouldn't keep them from helping George and those like him. George wasn't the first slave they had sheltered on his way to freedom in Canada and she dared say he would not be the last.

Louisa stirred the soup with a wistful air, thinking of tomorrow's lunch. The pickings would be sparse indeed without the soup. Then she glanced toward the enormous man at their table, thinking of everything their guest had suffered.

In a fit of shame, she pulled out a hunk of cheddar cheese wrapped in a moist cloth from the larder. It was her own, a special treat from Mrs. Emerson to thank Louisa for doing some embroidery. She rarely got to eat cheese because Father felt that cheese was immoral. After all, the milk was taken forcibly from the cow. With a decided thump, she put the entire piece of cheese on a plate for George.

She was rewarded when Marmee spied the plate. She smiled at Louisa, approval shining from her eyes.

George cut a chunk and paired it with a slice of bread and bit into it gratefully. He nodded his thanks when Louisa put the soup in front of him. He took the spoon and shoveled the thick soup into his mouth.

Marmee, ever practical, was making plans. "So you need to stay hidden for a few days?"

"Maybe even a week," George said, his shoulders hunched and his eyes on the bowl of soup. "The Conductor in Dedham didn't know when he'd be able to send my wife and daughters on. I know it's more danger for you . . ."

"Nonsense," Marmee and Bronson said in unison.

Bronson placed his large callused hand on George's shoulder. At first George flinched, then he relaxed. "My family and friends are prepared to make any sacrifice to protect our less fortunate brothers." Bronson looked to Marmee and Louisa for affirmation and they both nodded solemnly. In this, at least, the Alcott family was united. "We have a room for you in the barn," Bronson continued. "We'd like to have you in the house, but we have too many visitors. Most are sympathetic to our principles, but not everyone. The barn is safer for you."

"Whatever you say, Mr. Alcott," George said.

"The barn is old; it goes back to before the Revolution," Louisa explained. "It used to be across the road, but Father moved it nearer to the house. That's when he found a secret room where they used to hide guns. That's where you'll stay. We've made it ever so comfortable. Father put in a window for light, but it's up high so no one can see in."

"You'll be safe," Bronson interrupted Louisa's litany of amenities.

George held out his hand. "Thank you, sir. I can see I'm in the hands of a good man." He and Bronson shook solemnly as though they were settling a bargain.

"A good family," interrupted Louisa.

"We'll all be good together," laughed Marmee. "Louisa, come with me and we'll prepare our guest's bed."

Marmee made Louisa wrap a shawl around her shoulders. Holding a lantern, she opened the door outside and stepped into the rock garden. The night sky was full of stars, and despite the frigid air, they stopped to stare skyward for a moment.

"Brrrr, it's cold," Marmee said, rubbing her hands together. "What on earth were you doing outside instead of in your room, where I told you to stay?"

"I was upset," Louisa said, her eyes shifting to the ground. "I needed to be outside, where there was room enough for my temper."

Marmee reached out and stroked her hair. "When I'm away, you'd best not let your father know how often you go outside at night."

"You know?" Louisa asked, not really surprised. Marmee knew everything. That was why she was so necessary.

"Of course." She leaned over and kissed Louisa on the forehead. "And how like you, Louy, to go outside in a fit of pique and find someone who needs our help!"

An idea occurred to Louisa—if Marmee wouldn't stay for the family, she would never abandon a fugitive slave. "Marmee, you can't go now. Who will take care of George? And his family when they get here?"

"I don't want to leave. But our finances . . . you're the only one in the family who knows how desperate they are. I have to do something."

"But Marmee—you cannot go. Am I to take care of Beth, May, and Father? And now George?"

Marmee exhaled, and her breath hung for a moment in the air. "I hadn't counted on George. But I'll be taking May with me. And Beth will be a help to you."

There was a silence. Louisa broke it. "And Father?"

"The two of you are so different," Marmee said with a sigh. "But he loves you dearly. Just be patient and you'll be able to manage him."

Louisa made a rude snorting sound.

A smile flitted across Marmee's lips. "I'll write you often. You won't ever run out of advice from your Marmee."

"But . . ."

"Louisa May Alcott, please do as I ask. Take care of the family and the house while I am gone. You are the only one I can rely on."

Miserable, Louisa nodded. It might be impossible, but she couldn't let Marmee down.

CHAPTER THREE

"Girls' quarrels are soon over," returned her
mother, feeling a trifle ashamed of her own part in
this one, as well she might.

*L*ouisa sensed the thin sunlight of early morning on her face, but she refused to open her eyes. This was the best part of every day, when she was suspended between sleep and waking, before the press of chores and obligations usurped her time.

She stretched her legs, her feet draping over the end of the bed. Outside a woodpecker pecked on her wall, a familiar irritant. She banged on the wall and with a final indignant tap the bird moved on to another landing place.

Like tendrils of fog, the smell of one of Marmee's delicious omelets drifted under the ill-fitting door to Louisa's room. She inhaled deeply, anticipating how good they would taste. Suddenly, a weight landed on her chest and her eyes flew open.

Her latest acquisition, a tiger-eyed black kitten from a new litter at the Emersons', sat on her chest, preening himself. He nuzzled her chin and licked her cheek with his raspy tongue.

"Very well, Goethe," she said, scratching his head. "It's time to get up. But you mustn't let Marmee see that you slept in here. She doesn't approve." Louisa lifted the kitten off and dumped him on the floor.

A knock at the door was followed by Beth's gentle voice. "Louy, are you awake?"

Of Louisa's three sisters, Beth was the dearest to her and the one whose health she worried most about. This past winter had been particularly damp and Beth was still suffering the effects. How would fragile Beth take the news of Marmee leaving?

"Come in." The door opened and Goethe made a beeline to Beth. She was a favorite with all the cats. She stooped to rub his chin, looking sidelong at Louisa. "Gracious! It's not like you to still be abed at seven in the morning."

Beth was thirteen to Louisa's fifteen and a half, but her hair was always smooth and her light blue eyes never cried angry tears. The family called her the Angel in the House. As much as Louisa loved her, Beth made her feel more devilish than ever.

"I was up late, having adventures, while you were slugabed!" Louisa stretched her arms to the ceiling and yawned. "Did Marmee tell you about the slave I found?"

"From what I heard, he found us," Beth scolded gently. Shrinking into herself, she asked, "What is he like? Does he speak roughly?"

"Don't be so timid!" Louisa hopped out of bed and hugged her sister. "George is very sweet. He can read and write. Ironically, that has made his lot worse. His master wants him back and has put a high price on his head!"

Louisa reached into her closet and pulled out a shapeless linen dress. "I suppose I shouldn't wear cotton, in deference to his feelings," she said. Their father never wore cotton because it was the product of slave labor. In the past few years he had reluctantly agreed to let the girls wear secondhand clothes donated from relatives who didn't share Bronson Alcott's high-minded standards.

Beth wrinkled her nose. "Louy, I doubt that George will care. And that dress looks like a sack of potatoes."

Louisa burst out laughing and grabbed her usual day dress. "The cotton it is. Father's principles be damned!" she cried.

"Ssssh," Beth hissed. "Someone will hear."

"So?"

Abandoning the finer points of fabric choice, Beth focused on the new risk to the family. "Is hiding George more dangerous than the other slaves we've sheltered?" Beth's charitable nature was often at odds with her protective instincts about the family.

Louisa's words were smothered by the pinafore she was pulling over her head. "It doesn't matter, dear Beth. It's our duty regardless of the risk."

"You can say that because you aren't afraid of anything!" Beth cried. "The rest of us are not so bold."

Louisa's head popped up through the collar on her dress. "It's too early to disagree, Beth, so let's not."

"It's not like you to avoid a fight." Beth's smile was sly, almost a challenge.

"Let's argue after breakfast," Louisa said. "It smells delicious!" She was almost certain that Marmee hadn't told Beth her plans to leave. If she had, Beth wouldn't be in here talking about George.

Beth hesitated, then said with an embarrassed look on her face, "One of us is supposed to bring George breakfast."

"Ah, so now I see why you woke me up! You're afraid to do it!" Louisa said, with a mock glare at her sister.

"He's a stranger . . . and I'm . . ."

"I know, Beth." Louisa relented. "You're shy around new people, and I'm a beast to make you feel badly for it! I'll bring George food to break his fast. I don't mind. And later I'll introduce you so you don't need to be nervous." She pulled her nightcap off, revealing plaits so untidy and loose they could hardly be called braids.

"Oh, Louy, why don't you let me braid your hair at night? That's going to pull terribly when you try to brush it. Your hair is so thick and beautiful—and it's such a nice chestnut color, you should take better care with it."

Twisting her braids into a messy knot and pulling a loose net over her thick hair, Louisa said, "Beth, hush. Let's go."

Louisa pushed her sister out the door and followed her into the kitchen. Marmee stood at the stove, her back straight and her thick coils of hair fastened neatly about her head. Eight-year-old May sat at the table single-mindedly eating spoonfuls of cooked egg. Even though the family always began the day with the reading of a hymn, Father was nowhere to be seen.

"Good morning, Louisa," Marmee said. Her penetrating look warned Louisa not to mention her mother's plans in front of the younger girls. "Sit down and eat." She slid a large omelet from a cast-iron skillet onto Louisa's waiting plate.

Determined to show Marmee she had understood the unspoken message, Louisa made sure that May was preoccupied with her breakfast and asked quietly, "Should I take some food to the barn?"

"It's going to be a busy day, so you should eat first," Marmee said, rewarding Louisa's discretion with a nod of approval. "What is in the barn must stay hidden until you and I can talk to the Conductor."

"Me?" Louisa put her hand to her neck.

"It's time that you become more involved with our Railroad duties," Marmee said. Beth was busy eating and Marmee whispered to Louisa, "While I'm gone, someone has to take care of George and send him on his way." Louisa couldn't keep the dismay from her face. Marmee kissed her on the top of her head and said, "You're young, but you're also sensible."

Louisa let out a sigh of long suffering as another responsibility settled on her aching shoulders. But deep inside she felt a twinge of pride that Marmee trusted her to help with such important work. She fell to the omelet with a fierce appetite. "I thank goodness every morning for your cooking, Marmee," she said between forkfuls.

"You should be thanking the chickens," came her father's deep voice. He had stolen up on them from the back door, carrying some kindling for the stove. "We eat their eggs because they are freely given in exchange for the shelter and food we provide to them." Without ceremony he dropped the wood next to the stove. Marmee turned her back to him without a word and began cracking more eggs into a pan.

"Thank you, chickies," May said with her charming lisp.

"Very good, May," her father said.

"Well, Marmee makes the omelets taste delicious," Louisa pronounced.

"Of course," he said. He paused, then said in a deliberate way, his eyes fixed on his wife, "But when Marmee is gone, who will cook for us? Louisa, your cooking skills have greatly improved, but they aren't yet of your mother's caliber."

"Gone? What does he mean?" Beth asked, suddenly pale. "Where are you going, Marmee dear?"

Marmee turned slowly, glaring at Bronson. "Beth, don't be upset. I was going to tell you today."

"So you *are* going?" Beth cried.

"Marmee's going away!" May began to weep.

"Girls, I need you to be brave!" Turning to May, Marmee said, "May, you'll be coming with me, so there's no reason for you to moan."

Beth's words were nearly swallowed by her heaving sobs. "You're taking May and leaving us? What will we do without you?"

Marmee led Beth out of the kitchen, May following close on their heels, clamoring for more information.

Louisa stared daggers at her father. The brief alliance she had shared with him last night was shattered by the thoughtless way he had let the cat out of the bag. Marmee would have told Beth gently and helped her to accept the news.

"Why did you do that?" she demanded. "You should have known that Beth would be upset." She'd never spoken so disrespectfully to her father before.

"It's your mother who should be sorry," Bronson muttered. He sat down at the table and without warning he pounded his fist on the table. "If she hadn't conceived this plan, then we'd be eating a happy breakfast together as a family."

Louisa's jaw trembled with the effort of not saying what she wished to say. A sizzling on the stove and the briefest wisp of smoke distracted her. She rushed to save the burning omelet.

"Is that for me?" Bronson asked. "Your mother wouldn't feed me earlier."

Louisa couldn't resist. "No, Father. This is for our guest. You wouldn't eat your meal at his expense, would you? He has suffered so much more than you." She wrapped the plate in a cloth and deposited it in a basket.

"Since I'm not wanted here," Bronson said, pushing himself slowly up from the table, "I'll be in my study."

"Of course, Father," Louisa said, concentrating on packing George's meal. A few biscuits, some apples, and a jar of water completed the basket.

"Fasting is a good tool to focus the mind," he muttered. "I might write about that." His shoulders slumped, he ducked his head to go through the low doorway.

"Another essay that no one will buy," Louisa said under her breath. She banked the coals on the stove and slipped the handle of the basket over her arm.

Outside, the spring air was cold and there was frost on the grass. Louisa hurried through the garden to the barn. She unlatched the barn doors and dragged them open.

Inside the barn was dark. Although stalls lined the back of the barn, there were no animals here. Her father did not agree with keeping animals in captivity. He likened the use of animals for work to slavery. Louisa wasn't sure she agreed, and she had often reflected that whenever the Alcott family moved her father had accepted the use of cart horses.

The stall at the end of the row was much narrower than the others, but no one would suspect that it concealed a hidden room. She stepped inside the stall. "George!" she called softly. "It's me, Louisa Alcott."

After a moment, a hidden door swung open. It was so cunningly disguised that even if you knew it was there, you might not find the secret way of unlocking it. Inside it was cramped but adequate for a grown man. The ceiling was very high, to the height of the barn roof. A bed, a small set of drawers, a chamber pot, and a stack of books were the only amenities.

"Good morning, Miss Louisa," George said. He looked exhausted, and Louisa feared he had not slept. He was wearing a discarded shirt of her father's, and even though Bronson was a powerfully built man, the shirt was stretched across George's shoulders.

Cheerfully she said, "My mother's omelets shouldn't be eaten cold, so eat up!"

George took the basket and began to eat Marmee's food with relish.

"I hope you were comfortable last night," she said.

"Yes, thank you," George said, swallowing his food.

"My mother has to talk to the others on the Railroad. Will you be all right here for a few hours?"

"I'd rather be useful to your family." He nodded eagerly. "I can help around the farm."

"I know. But you need to stay out of sight. Get some rest. Maybe you would like something to read?"

"It's awfully dark in here."

"Ah, you haven't seen the windows yet," Louisa said. She showed him a crank attached to the wall. When he turned it, a set of shutters opened near the eaves to reveal three narrow windows. Light poured in, illuminating the small room.

"That's clever," he said.

"My father invented them," Louisa said. "When my parents began helping fugitives, we added the furniture but my father couldn't imagine a space without light. Or a night that you couldn't spend reading by candlelight without fear of discovery. No matter how bright your candle or lantern, if the shutters are closed, it can't be seen from the outside. We've tested it." She paused a moment, then said, "Would you like me to lend you a book?"

He reached into his knapsack and brought out a well-used Bible. "I have one, Miss."

"An excellent book," Louisa agreed. "But I also have some novels, if you prefer a change."

"I would like that, Miss."

Louisa smiled at him. "I have a perfect one in mind. I'll bring it when I come back with your dinner. I'm not sure how you ate in Virginia, but here we have our main meal around

noon. You can go out into the barn, but don't go outside yet."
She waited until he nodded his promise.

She let herself out of the barn. A farmer was passing by on
the road and he waved a cautious greeting. With the exception
of their philosopher friends, the rest of the inhabitants of
Concord were farmers who didn't trust men who thought for a
living. Or, in Bronson Alcott's case, for no living at all.

Louisa waved back, careful to seem casual as she shoved
the barn doors closed. No one must suspect that the Alcotts
had a secret in their barn. She hated to think ill of their
neighbors, but George had said there was a price on his head.
Who knew what people might do for money? Or to show how
law-abiding they were? Or even just to make trouble for the
eccentric Bronson Alcott?

She returned to the kitchen and found her mother standing by the sink lost in thought, her eyes fixed on the terraced
hillside behind the house. "Marmee?"

Her mother didn't answer.

"Marmee," Louisa repeated. "Is Beth all right?"

"Ah, Louy, I'm sorry. I didn't hear you come in." Marmee
started scrubbing at the frying pan as if it were the most
important thing in the world. "Beth is fine. She has the gift of
acceptance."

"Maybe she could teach it to me," Louisa said.

Marmee smiled ruefully. "A lesson I too could learn. How
is George this morning?"

"He's fine. He liked your omelet."

"That's good." Marmee nodded in satisfaction. "Now, help me with the dishes. I still have a dozen tasks to do if I am to leave on tomorrow's train."

"Tomorrow!" Louisa staggered back. "But that's so soon."

"'If it were done when 'tis done, then 'twere well it were done quickly,'" she said with a hint of her usual dark sense of humor.

"You're no Lady Macbeth," Louisa said hotly.

"This morning your father might disagree." She sighed. "We're out of sorts with each other. I've not been tactful with him, I'm afraid. Last night I picked that quarrel. How I wish I could control my temper!"

Louisa rubbed a dish dry with a rag, then picked up another. "Marmee, I was very rude to Father myself a few minutes ago," she confessed. "I know he didn't mean to shock Beth like that, but it was poorly done." She braced herself for the scolding Marmee was sure to administer. Criticizing her father was something her mother never tolerated. To her surprise, Marmee dropped the heavy iron pot into the sink. It landed with a reverberating thud and water sloshed over the sink rim onto the floor.

"He knew exactly what he was doing," she said. "He thought I would change my mind rather than see Beth cry."

"Marmee! He wouldn't!" But Louisa was running the scene over in her head. He had deliberately dragged Marmee's departure into the conversation. And Father rarely said anything by accident.

Mopping up the spilled water, Marmee's eyes filled with angry tears. "Now there, I'm doing it again. I must have more compassion. Your father will miss me terribly, I know. But he's acting as though I have a choice." She glanced up at Louisa, so forlorn that on impulse Louisa put her arms around Marmee and held her for several moments. It was the first time Marmee had let Louisa comfort her. And while Louisa was proud, it was unsettling to be Marmee's support instead of the other way around.

"Marmee, don't worry," she murmured. "You go earn money to keep us and I'll take charge here."

After a few moments, Marmee regained her self-control. Sniffing, she said, "Louisa, thank you, dear. I knew I could count on you." She kissed Louisa on the forehead and assumed her usual businesslike air. "Now, about our guest. First you must go to Mr. Emerson and tell him about George."

Louisa's jaw dropped. "Mr. Emerson is part of the Railroad, too?" Ralph Waldo Emerson was a world-renowned philosopher and writer. He was Bronson's closest friend and had often lent the family money when his largesse had meant the difference between starving and eating. He also possessed an excellent library from which Louisa was at liberty to borrow.

"Mr. Emerson supports the cause even if he does not participate in the actual work of the Railroad. But he must know about George—if only so that he can be careful about visiting the house. His work is too important for him to compromise himself. He has a reputation to maintain."

"Not like the Alcotts," Louisa retorted.

"No," Marmee agreed. "I am proud to say that principle will always trump social respectability in this house."

Louisa watched her mother's face closely, unable to decide if she were serious or not. In a small voice, she said, "Marmee, I rather like that about us."

"I do, too." Marmee lowered her voice. "Louy, while I'm away, you must know that whenever Mr. Emerson visits, he leaves money on the mantelpiece behind the clock. If he comes, you have to get the money before your father does. You'll need it when I'm gone."

Louisa stared at her mother in consternation. "I knew Mr. Emerson lent us the funds to buy this house, but he gives us money, too?"

"But very tactfully. He doesn't want to embarrass your father." Marmee shrugged. "Now off with you, because after the Emersons' you'll need to find Henry."

"Henry?" Louisa's heart beat a bit faster.

"Yes, he'll be of the greatest help to you while I'm gone. There's nothing he wouldn't do for the Railroad."

"Of course. We'll have to work closely together, I'm sure," Louisa said, trying to sound matter-of-fact. But she could see from Marmee's indulgent smile that Marmee wasn't fooled.

"Henry is fifteen years your senior," Marmee warned. "He's too old for you."

"Mother!" Louisa felt the flush rise in her cheeks and she wished for one moment that Marmee's eyes weren't so sharp.

"Never mind, my dear. Your calf-love is safe in his hands. Henry's a good man, not one to tease you. You're only young once." She kissed Louisa on the cheek. "Now go."

As Louisa pulled her shawl around her shoulders, she thought how her youth was mostly being devoured by hard work and poverty. But not today.

Today she was saving a fugitive.

And she would have the chance to talk with Henry David Thoreau.

CHAPTER FOUR

*The dim, dusty room, with . . . the wilderness of
books in which she could
wander where she liked, made the library a region
of bliss to her.*

*D*eep in thought, Louisa stepped into the road without
paying attention.

"Watch out!" A man on a black horse cantered along the
road directly in her path. Louisa fell against the gate into the
dust. The rider pulled back on the reins and his horse wheeled to
a halt, rearing, its front legs pawing the air above Louisa's head.

Cursing, the rider dismounted and threw his reins around the gatepost. "Are you blind? I could have killed you!"

Louisa patted herself and realized that she was bruised but not broken. However, her sharp tongue had not suffered any damage. "You should look where you are going! What kind of idiot rides that fast along a main road in town?"

Squinting her eyes against the sun, Louisa tried to get the measure of the stranger. She couldn't see his face clearly, but she had earned enough money as a seamstress to know his clothes were expensively tailored. He wore a top hat covered with dust from the road and his pale hair spilled out from beneath the brim onto his thick neck. Not young, but not old, perhaps in his early thirties.

"I was in a hurry," he replied tersely. In his voice, she heard a hint of the South.

"Hardly an excuse for running me down," Louisa replied. She knew she was being impertinent, but her bottom hurt from the fall. With dismay, she saw her skirt had a rip.

He reached out to help her up. "I rather think you stepped in front of me. This was your fault."

Feeling ridiculous and at a disadvantage, Louisa clambered to her feet, ignoring his outstretched hand. "I disagree. You were riding recklessly. This road is used by children and livestock, all moving at reasonable rates of speed. If you aren't careful the next time, you'll kill someone."

He took a deep breath, as if to control his temper. Louisa recognized the technique; she often used it herself with varying degrees of success. "Young lady, I beg your pardon," he said, his tone suddenly courteous. "What I did was unforgivable."

"I do pardon you," she said, knowing she should apologize in her turn, but he had put her back up.

His lips twitched, perhaps to resist smiling at her rudeness. "My name is Russell Finch," he said. She inclined her head, acknowledging the introduction but still wary. In her experience people did not go from rude to ingratiating without a hidden motive.

"I'm from Concord originally," he said. "I'd be very grateful if you can tell me where Henry Thoreau might be found."

"Henry Thoreau?" she repeated, eyeing Finch. She didn't like the look of this stranger. He could ask her until doomsday before he would get any information from her about Henry. "I've heard the name, but I don't think I know him."

His pale gray eyes stared her down in return. "Really? Unless Concord has gotten much bigger in my absence, I find that hard to believe."

She shrugged and started walking, leaving him behind. She heard him mount his horse and come up behind her at a decorous pace. "Well, thank you, Miss . . ." He paused, looking down at her from the saddle. "I don't think I heard your name."

"That's because I didn't tell you," she replied, keeping her eyes forward.

There was a long pause and then he suddenly shook the reins and kicked his horse. Louisa coughed from the dust thrown up by his galloping horse. She scowled after his disappearing figure, wishing she had been even more discourteous.

Careful to look in both directions, she crossed the road and made quick work of the quarter mile to the Emersons' house. At the white fence, she paused, looking up at the familiar and beloved house. Mr. Emerson lived in a proper home, with servants and carpeting and stoves that warmed every room without filling them with smoke. Best of all was his library.

She climbed the steps to the front door and let herself inside. Long ago the family had insisted Louisa treat the house as her own. How she wished it were! The front hall was filled with paintings and statues, with pale flowered paper on the walls. Lidian Emerson, Mr. Emerson's wife, had delicate tastes, and she ordered the paper from a fancy store in Boston. Louisa loved how the pattern repeated across the walls, never varying, always predictable. She and her sisters had painted designs on their walls, with uneven results.

Mr. Emerson's library was to the right and she knocked softly.

"Who is it?" The familiar deep voice sounded wary.

"Louisa," she answered.

He responded at once. "Come in."

She pushed open the door and stepped into her favorite room, her sanctuary and refuge from the chaos of daily life at the Alcotts'. Here, she could read as much as she pleased and no one ever bothered her. It was also Mr. Emerson's office and even as a little girl, she had been one of the few people he tolerated in the room while he was working. Every time she came into the room she glanced at the sofa with the legs shaped like elephants. She smiled, remembering how she used to burrow into its depths, intent on discovering the secrets in the novels of Sir Walter Scott and Charles Dickens.

In the center of the room, seated at a round mahogany table, Mr. Emerson was writing in his sprawling illegible way, fitting only five or six words to a line. From long practice, she waited until he finished his thought. She admired his profile as he wrote. Not quite fifty, Emerson was an imposing figure of a man who carried himself like a statesman.

With a flourish, he finished the sentence and pushed away his morocco leather writing pad. His eyes lifted, and he smiled at the sight of her.

"Louisa, my dear, thank goodness it's you. I thought it might be that Edith Whittaker woman."

"Ah," she said, understanding his suspicious greeting. "Has she been a frequent visitor?"

"Too frequent. While it is gratifying to be so admired, it can be tiring." He looked at her slyly, peering down his large nose that somehow fit his face to perfection. "I wager she has not yet worn out her welcome in your father's study!"

Louisa didn't hide her answering grin. "Not yet. At least not with Father. Marmee, however, could do with a little less of Miss Whittaker's company . . ."

Emerson chuckled. "And how are you?" he asked. "Have you already finished the book I gave you?"

"No, sir," she said. "*Jane Eyre* is so wonderful that I am rationing it. I read a chapter a day, unless I have lost my temper. Then I must wait another day. At this rate, I may never finish."

"That's your father's preaching," he chided. "Self-denial is all very well, but not at the expense of your true self. Your temper is part of what makes you a splendid person."

Louisa tilted her head to one side. "So you think I should finish the novel?"

He grinned wickedly and his deep-set eyes glinted with enjoyment. "I'm trying to give you a sound philosophical reason for doing so."

"Just in case I have to justify my actions?" She felt her own smile broaden. "I'll do exactly as you say, particularly as I'm dying to find out what happens to Jane and Mr. Rochester."

"But if you don't need a new book, why are you here, my dear?" he asked, gesturing to the chair opposite him.

"Marmee sent me." She took her seat. "Last night I found a 'package' who is to stay with us for a few days while his family makes the journey North."

Emerson's grin faded and he leaned back in his chair. "I see," he said, in a flat voice.

Louisa had long ago decided that Mr. Emerson was the finest man she knew. But there was one part of his personality that she could not reconcile herself to: Dedicated as he was to the freedom of all men, how could he not be involved with the work of the Underground Railroad? His wife, Lidian, and his closest friends were active participants, but Emerson held himself above the fray.

There was a long moment of uncomfortable silence. "Mother thought you ought to know," Louisa said finally.

"Your mother is a wonderful and caring person," Emerson said thoughtfully. "But I wonder if this is one burden too many for her. How will you feed him?"

Louisa sighed. "Marmee is going to New Hampshire for the summer to work. So it falls to me."

Emerson's eyes rested on her with kindness mixed with exasperation. "What are they thinking?" he muttered to himself. Louder, he said, "Let's dispense with these foolish circumlocutions and speak frankly. What if you are caught sheltering a fugitive? Your father could be prosecuted—maybe even you, too. Then what would become of you all?"

"It's a risk we accept," Louisa said. "It's not enough to just talk about the abolition of slavery; I think that we must also act to make it so." She cringed a little, watching his face for his reaction to what could be interpreted as criticism of Emerson himself. She breathed easier when he began to laugh.

"Louisa, you are the daughter of both your parents. You have your father's idealism with your mother's practicality. How old are you now? Only fifteen and already a force to be reckoned with."

Louisa's face grew warm. At home she was never praised like this. Even her mother's encouraging words were often tinged with her father's disapproval.

Emerson went on, "Tell Lidian about your slave and that Mrs. Alcott is going away. She will help all she can. Especially if there are children." A brief shadow crossed his face then flitted away. But Louisa knew he had been thinking of his own little boy, Waldo, who had died of scarlet fever six years earlier. Waldo was never far from his thoughts.

He waved his hand toward the back of the house. "Queenie is somewhere about. I'm sure she'll be of great help to you." Despite his irreverent nickname for her, Emerson was very proud of his regal second wife.

Taking his words for her dismissal, Louisa left the study by the door to the dining room. It was empty, as were the kitchen and the parlor. She listened and thought she heard a rumble of voices upstairs. She hurried up the narrow back stairs. As Louisa rounded the landing where the stairs doubled back on themselves, she stopped short.

Lidian Emerson stood at the top, her back pressed against the wall. A man leaned over her, his hand braced on the wall above her head. They were talking in low voices, his lips near to her ear. He was dressed in clothes the color of the woods. It was Henry Thoreau.

When Lidian saw Louisa, she pushed Henry away, almost as if her hand completed the action without her willing it. She stood in a patch of sunlight coming in from a window set high in the wall. Although near fifty years old, she was considered a beauty, with wide-spaced brown eyes and porcelain skin. She was the kind of person who couldn't tolerate any untidiness and even the part of her thick dark hair surrendered to her quest for order.

"Louisa!" Henry said, stepping away from Lidian.

"Louisa," Lidian said in the exact same moment. "I wasn't expecting you." She smoothed her already perfect hair, and turned away from Henry to face Louisa.

Louisa's eyes traveled between the two, wondering at their odd behavior. They were acting as if Henry shouldn't be there. But when Henry wasn't writing he earned his living doing odd jobs, including tending the Emersons' garden and minding their chickens. When Emerson had gone to Europe the year before, he had asked Henry to stay in the house and take care of Lidian and the children.

"A 'package' arrived by rail last night," Louisa said, relishing the conspiratorial language. "Mr. Emerson said I should tell you."

"What kind of package?" Lidian asked.

Since Louisa didn't actually know any other Railroad terms and there was no one to overhear, she answered straightforwardly. "A solitary man, but there are more to come." Louisa explained about George's circumstances. "Mr. Emerson thought you would be able to help with the children."

With a sharp nod, Lidian said, "I'll put some clothes aside and start gathering the supplies they'll need."

"Where is he staying?" Henry asked. "In the barn?"

Louisa nodded.

"I'll come back with you and meet him."

"You were my next stop."

"Be careful . . . both of you." Lidian warned.

"Of course, my dear," Henry said. His hand started toward her but she moved away.

Louisa frowned and turned to hurry down the stairs. Henry followed her outside, moving as effortlessly as she did. They had always had that in common—neither was happy sitting still for long, unless they were writing. It would have been better if she had found him some distance away so they would have longer to talk. Her best memories of childhood were of following Henry into the woods around Walden Pond.

"Louisa," Henry began. "About what you saw earlier . . ."

"What?" Louisa answered, brow slightly furrowed. "I didn't see anything."

Henry's face was flushed and he ran his hand through his thick black hair. "I was talking with Lidian . . . Mrs. Emerson."

A twinge of unease stirred in Louisa's stomach. She didn't want Henry to be confiding any secrets to her. "You're very kind to her. I think she's had a hard life. It's not easy to be married to a philosopher if you aren't trained to it," she said, thinking of her mother.

Although he clearly had intended to talk about something else, Henry couldn't resist ribbing her. "You think you'd be a suitable wife to a philosopher? You'd never stop pacing around the house or having arguments for the fun of it. There'd never be a moment's peace."

"That's not true," Louisa shot back. "I understand the need for conversation and high-minded thought. And you forget, I'd be writing, too. Lidian told me once that she thought of writing, but she's forgotten that in her quest to be the perfect housewife."

"You're unfair to her. She is a great help to Emerson in his work as well as managing the house and children. He doesn't appreciate her. Louisa, her life is harder than you think."

Louisa patted Henry's arm, as if patronizing him would keep him from admiring his best friend's wife. "I'm glad she has a *friend* to sustain her through her struggles." Her tone lightly underlined the word "friend."

"You make her sound pathetic. She's really very joyous," he said, tugging at his necktie. "And very lovely."

"For a woman of her age," Louisa conceded.

"She's only fifteen years older than I am," he said, starch in his voice.

Louisa felt the heat rush to the roots of her hair. If Henry wanted to confide in her, she was going to tell him exactly what she thought.

"She's Mr. Emerson's wife," she said. "Our patron, your friend."

"I know," he moaned, rubbing the bridge of his nose furiously. "I've admired her for so long. From a distance," he insisted. "She is Waldo's wife and must be above reproach. But today she was all of a sudden approachable and so kind to me. . . . I don't know why I'm talking to you like this. Sometimes I forget how young you are." He gave Louisa a sharp look. "You must say nothing!"

"I don't gossip," Louisa said, bristling at the suggestion. After an excruciating minute, she trusted her voice enough. "Why are we talking about Mrs. Emerson?" she asked. "We have so many more interesting topics to discuss."

Henry was at a loss for words. Finally he spread out his callused hands. "You choose, Miss Alcott."

For the first time, his rough manners failed to charm Louisa. But there was something he needed to know, she decided. "There was a stranger asking for you not long ago, on this very road."

"What manner of stranger?" Henry brought his eyebrows together in a scowl. Louisa smiled to herself. There was a reason he was called the most cantankerous man in Concord: He did not like unexpected visitors.

"Do you mean was he a naturalist, a philosopher, or a curiosity seeker?" Louisa teased.

"Well?" Henry asked.

She chewed on her bottom lip, recalling every moment of her meeting. "He was rude and he knocked me down with his horse. And when I refused to admit knowing you . . ."

With a theatrical smack of his head, Thoreau said, "What, denied by Louisa Alcott? How shall I bear it?"

She glared at him, but within herself she didn't mind. "He galloped away without so much as a thank you. His name was Robin. No, Hawk. No . . . Finch! That was it. Russell Finch."

Henry stopped dead in the street. "Finch is in town?"

"You know him?"

"We were at school together. We had a falling-out." His tone warned her not to ask any questions.

"If he had a falling-out with you," Louisa said, "I'm glad I was impertinent to him."

A smile touched Henry's lips and disappeared. "He left town years ago." His deep voice dropped another half octave. "I heard he's done quite well for himself in a new career, which is troubling for us . . ." His gaze focused on a distant horizon and his voice trailed off.

"Henry?" Louisa demanded. "Henry, you should give up your essays and start writing stories—you are very good at creating suspense! Why is his new career so alarming?"

His eyes caught hers and she could see the warning and the worry in them. "He's a slave catcher."

CHAPTER FIVE

"It's always so. Amy has all the fun
and I have all the work.
It isn't fair, oh, it isn't fair!" cried Jo passionately.

"Beth, please may I borrow your gloves?" May asked. Her small trunk was open wide and there were clothes strewn pell-mell about the small bedroom. Beth sat on May's bed, retrieving dresses and nightgowns and folding them neatly. "I'll need them more than you because there will be social occasions at the resort," May went on. "Marmee says the guests are ever so smart."

At eight, May was the pet of the family and had the enviable knack of always getting what she wanted. The youngest Alcott girl shouldn't be the one traveling while her elder sister packed for her, Louisa thought. "Don't give your gloves to her," she warned Beth from the doorway. "After May uses them for the whole summer you'll never get a day's wear out of them again."

"You're just jealous, Louisa," May retorted. "Because Marmee picked me to go and not you!" May tossed her blond curls and sniffed. She had read in a romantic novel that this was ladylike.

"Jealous?" Louisa laughed out loud. "You little ninny. You're only going because you couldn't stay at home without Marmee!"

As if Louisa had stuck May with a pin, May started howling.

"Louisa!" Beth interrupted May's wail. "May, take them. I won't need them." She passed her little sister a limp pair of white cloth gloves. "And while you're away, Louisa and I are going to have a lovely summer; she's going to finish the novel she's been so secretive about and I'm going to play the piano, and we're both going to take care of Father."

"That sounds very nice, Beth," May said graciously, nodding with the manners of someone much more mature.

"I promise I'll think of you often. When I have the time, of course."

Louisa growled, "Fine, let her have the gloves. Otherwise she'll just charm Marmee into buying her a new pair that we can't afford!" She turned on her heel and ran down the stairs, her toes barely touching the steps. She couldn't stay to help others pack for their adventures. Not while she remained at home in the dullest town in the world.

"Louisa!" Marmee emerged from the parlor, carrying a small pile of books. Louisa stopped short on the third stair from the bottom.

"Yes, Marmee?" she asked, just barely keeping her frustration out of her voice.

"Is May ready yet? The boy will be here to fetch our trunks any minute now."

Glancing longingly at the door, Louisa said, "Not yet, Marmee." She looked back to the anxious expression on her mother's face. "But almost."

"Tell her to hurry. These are the last of what needs to be packed in my trunk." She handed the books up to Louisa. "Then buckle it up, please," Marmee said, already turning away, consulting her list. Over her shoulder she said, "I'll ask your father to carry it downstairs."

Louisa trudged back up to her parents' bedroom. The trunk stood in the middle of the worn carpet, its open top like a crocodile's mouth. She tossed the books inside and fastened the leather strap. Pulling hard enough to leave a mark on her hands, she told herself that her tears were from pain and not envy.

After checking that May was in the final stage of her packing, Louisa went downstairs to find Marmee. She followed the sound of voices to her father's study. Glancing about the hall to be sure she was unobserved, she sidled up to the study door, pressing her body close to the wall.

"So now you need my help?" Louisa heard her father say in the voice of a petulant little boy.

"Bronson, please, let's not argue again. We've been through this already." Marmee's voice was exasperated but cajoling. Louisa moved closer so she could peek through the slightly ajar door. Marmee stood close to Bronson, his back to her. Pressing her cheek against his broad back, Marmee circled his torso with her arms.

His neck and shoulders stiff, Bronson said, "You are making a fool of me. Everyone thinks I can't support the family and must send my wife out to work."

Louisa's eyebrows lifted high; why shouldn't they think that?

"Dear heart, I am going to earn money for the family, yes, but who else could I trust to take care of our daughters? I rely on you," Marmee assured him.

Louisa sighed for Marmee's mild response. Why didn't she scold him? Tell him that it was his fault that the family would be split up?

Marmee gently turned Bronson around to face her. "I will miss you quite terribly."

It was the right thing to say. He drew her close to him. "The summer nights won't be the same without you," he murmured, smiling down at Marmee. In a flash, Louisa appreciated how good-looking her father was. Perhaps that was why her mother put up with all his failings. He pressed his lips to Marmee's in a long kiss; she leant against him as though her knees wouldn't support her.

Suddenly embarrassed, Louisa started to back away. A knock at the door was a welcome distraction. She darted down the hall, away from the study, calling, "I'll answer it!"

The house had eight doors to the outside, but this knock came from the main door facing the road. Henry had warned her to be especially careful while Finch was in town, so she stopped herself from flinging it open as she usually did. Bracing the door with her booted foot, she opened it just a crack.

A boy waited on the steps. "I'm here for the baggage, miss." He gestured to his cart parked next to their gate.

The next few moments were chaotic. May had to reopen her trunk twice to put in her special colored pencils and then her favorite doll.

"What have you been doing all this time?" Louisa asked, not hiding her irritation. "Those are your favorite things. They should have been the first things packed."

"But then she would miss them too soon," Beth laughed.

May threw herself at Louisa's waist and hugged her tight. "Louy, I'm sorry for being so rude. Don't be cross with me, please? I wish you could come, too."

Over May's head, Louisa glared at Beth. Louisa knew perfectly well who had prompted this charming apology. But it required a harder heart than Louisa's to rebuff May.

"I love you, May." Louisa adjusted May's bonnet and tugged on the hem of her dress.

"Do I look pretty?" May asked.

"As pretty as one of your pictures," Louisa assured her.

"That's very pretty indeed," May said complacently.

"Don't be vain," Louisa said automatically. She scowled at the smile on Beth's face.

Downstairs, Marmee looked fine in her burgundy traveling suit with a black bonnet trimmed with ribbons to match. It was a hand-me-down, as were all their clothes, but it had been little worn by its previous owner, Marmee's sister-in-law. When she pulled on her thin gloves, Louisa and Beth nodded in approval. "I have to look respectable for my new position," she told them.

"You look lovely, Marmee," Beth said, her lower lip trembling and her eyes filling with tears. "But I'm feeling too selfish to give you up. "

"Beth, dear, give me a hug." Marmee held Beth close and whispered in her ear. Whatever she said, Louisa noted, cheered

Beth enough that the tears disappeared. "Now lie down. I heard you coughing last night. I want you to promise that while I'm away you will rest."

Her voice muffled by Marmee's bodice, Beth promised.

"Good," Marmee said with an approving nod. "Louisa can walk me to the train."

"What about Father?" Louisa asked, just then realizing that her father had disappeared once he brought the trunks downstairs.

"We've said our farewells already." Marmee's eyes went anxiously toward the study.

After settling Beth comfortably on the sofa with a book at hand, Louisa followed Marmee out the door. May was already running ahead toward town. They began walking, passing the Emersons' house on their left. Marmee checked the watch she wore on a chain around her neck. "We have just enough time to meet with Mr. Pryor."

"The tavern keeper?" Louisa asked, surprised. Except for some medicinal brandy, the Alcotts forbade any alcoholic spirits in the house.

Marmee nodded, her face solemn. "He's the Conductor for Concord. We take our orders from him."

"But I've never seen you ever talk to him," Louisa said.

"As members of the Temperance Society, we wouldn't be likely to, would we?" Marmee answered with a twinkle in her eye. "No one would suspect that we are working together."

"Does Mr. Pryor know about the slave catcher?"

Marmee nodded. "I sent him a message. He replied that we should keep George well hidden." She snorted, "As if we need to be told that!" She tucked Louisa's hand under her arm and they turned onto the Common, skirting the obelisk, a monument to the Revolutionary War's Battle of Concord. "But he needs to meet you. Any future messages will come to you."

"Not to Father?"

"I don't want you to bother him unnecessarily," Marmee said, blinking rapidly as if to hold back tears. "Of course, if George is in danger, go to your father. Otherwise, I am certain you can handle any situation."

Louisa's eyes were fixed on the skipping figure of May ahead of them. She thought of all the things that might go wrong. How could Marmee leave her with so much responsibility? Marmee's confidence in Louisa didn't make what she was asking any fairer.

"You can count on me," Louisa said. Her measured tone seemed to please her mother.

May came running back. "Marmee, may I have a penny to buy some candy for the train ride?"

Opening her small purse, Marmee put a penny in May's outstretched hand. "Go buy your candy and we'll meet you there." Marmee watched May run down the street, dodging pedestrians, until she entered J. W. Wolcott's. The general store was a favorite destination for every child in town.

Marmee's steps slowed as they approached the Wright Tavern, a sturdy red clapboard building with black trim on the edge of the common. The tavern had been an important rally-ing point for the Minutemen back in 1775, but not much had happened there since.

Marmee walked past the front door to the alley on the far side of the tavern. Glancing about the street, she chose a moment when no one was paying them any notice and pulled Louisa into the alley. Marmee slipped through the back door of the tavern, Louisa close on her heels. A half dozen cases of whiskey almost blocked their way. Mr. Pryor must have received a shipment early this morning, she thought.

Louisa's eyes explored the tavern, taking in every detail. At this hour, the tavern was empty of customers. Mr. Pryor was rubbing down the bar with a cloth. He was of medium height and wore a bright white shirt tucked into his workaday black trousers. His nose had been broken at least once, Louisa noticed.

Marmee coughed and caught Mr. Pryor's attention. He looked at her sharply and said, "You shouldn't be here. We can't be seen together." He hurried to the front door to lock it tight.

"My train leaves in three-quarters of an hour. In my absence my daughter Louisa is taking care of our package."

His quick glance took in all of Louisa, from her scuffed boots to her untidy hair, then dismissed her. "She's too young."

"I don't have a choice," Marmee snapped. "But Louisa is very responsible for her age."

"Does she understand the risks?" Mr. Pryor asked, his face sour as if he sucked on a lime.

"Of course," Marmee said.

"I was the first to meet George," Louisa added. "He's my responsibility."

Pryor hissed. "No names!"

Louisa pressed her lips together in a flat line. Marmee gave her elbow a comforting squeeze. Pryor went on, "I'd be happier if your package was safely on his way."

"When will the other packages arrive?" Marmee asked.

"Four or five days. We'll just have to keep him well hidden until then." He fixed Louisa with a stern stare. "So you, Miss Louisa, should avoid any other chance meetings with that slave catcher."

"I will."

"And tell your pet philosopher to avoid your house for the time being."

"Do you mean Henry?" Louisa asked.

"No names!" He glowered at her. "I run a tight ship."

"Oh, I'm sorry," Louisa said, just managing not to clap her hand over her mouth.

"Those two have a bad history. Your slave catcher would like nothing better than to turn us all in, just to spite our friend."

"What happened between them?" Louisa asked. Her mother frowned and glanced at her watch, but didn't interrupt.

"I don't know the story. I heard there was a woman involved." Pryor shrugged. "There always is."

Marmee gave Louisa a quick concerned glance, but Louisa kept her expression stoic. Apparently Henry had a knack of getting into trouble because of women. When she had time, Louisa was going to have to reevaluate her regard for him.

Pryor, unaware of all that was going on in Louisa's head, was still talking. "The catcher left town about five years ago. I heard he was a just a few steps ahead of the sheriff."

Marmee was fingering her watch. "We must go," she said.

Louisa wanted to know more. "Just one minute, Marmee," she begged. "What did Finch do to run afoul of the law?" In her mind she was really asking, "What is this man capable of?"

"Nothing serious. Some importation without taxation," Pryor said with a chuckle.

"Smuggling," Marmee summed up in a word, nostrils flaring and her mouth pinched.

"What's a little smuggling between friends? It's harmless," Pryor said. "Staying on the right side of the law is bad for business."

"Not for everyone," Marmee said with the prim air inherited from one of Boston's most straitlaced families. "We do not approve of lawbreaking."

"So what are you doing with the Railroad?" Pryor asked, raising his bushy eyebrows.

"That's a matter of principle." Marmee's voice was proud. Proud enough to rankle Pryor.

"And what principle absolves the Alcotts from paying their bills, Mrs. Alcott?"

Marmee stiffened. "Good day, Mr. Pryor," she said in an icy voice. Taking Louisa by the elbow, she pulled her out of the tavern's back door. In the alley, she said angrily, "How dare he say such a thing?" Her color was high and her dark eyes hard.

"It's true, though, Marmee," Louisa said. Between Marmee and herself, she thought, there should be complete honesty. "It's only through the intervention of kind people like Mr. Emerson and your family that Papa is a free man."

Marmee shook this argument off like a dog shook water off his fur. "Well, Pryor's a fine one to talk. When he took over the tavern, it was about to fail. But now it's a thriving business. Even the best businessman can't manage that."

Louisa stepped closer, leaning in to catch every word. "What do you mean?" Louisa asked.

"Did you see that stack of crates? Delivered off the back of a wagon in the middle of the night. He doesn't pay the duty on all his liquor," Marmee retorted. "It's how he keeps his prices lower than every other drinking establishments' in town. It's an open secret." She glanced at her watch. "I cannot miss this train. Let's find May." She set off down the alley.

Louisa looked from the tavern door to Marmee's outraged back marching down the alley. Who knew so much was happening beneath the surface in Concord? Louisa needed to pay closer attention.

As Louisa emerged on the street, Marmee was already entering the general store seven or eight doors down. Louisa started to follow when a hand grabbed her arm.

"So we meet again, young lady," a voice said. "Or should I say Miss Alcott?" He pushed her a few steps back into the shadow of the alley.

Louisa looked up the hand, along the arm, and into the mocking face of Mr. Finch.

CHAPTER SIX

*Jo would have gladly run away, if she could, but
she was perched aloft on the steps, and he stood at
the foot, a lion in the path, so she had to stay and
brave it out.*

"Let me go, Mr. Finch," Louisa said, trying unsuccessfully to pull her arm away. The odious man grinned at her, relishing her discomfiture. She could see passersby crossing in front of the alley; she had only to call and help would be forthcoming. But she preferred to solve her own problems. Using skills learned from years of playing with neighbor boys,

Louisa kicked Finch hard in the shin with her booted toe. He cried out and released her arm.

"Oh, I'm sorry." Louisa asked sweetly, "Did I hurt you?"

With a hostile look, he shook his knee as though it was numb. "Not at all," he muttered. He inhaled deeply, then managed to speak more pleasantly. "What a pleasure to see you again. I've learned quite a lot about you and your family since we met yesterday."

"Not the least of which is my name," Louisa agreed politely, proud of how level her voice was. She was face-to-face with the enemy. Louisa must outwit and outthink Finch if she were to save her fugitive slave.

"I've discovered the Alcotts are among the leading abolitionists in town. Second only to Henry Thoreau. So it's interesting that you pretended not to know him."

Better to admit what he already knew, Louisa decided. She opened her eyes very wide. "Oh, did you mean *that* Henry Thoreau? Of course I know Mr. Thoreau. He's a close friend of the family."

"He's not easy to find—I don't suppose you'll tell me where he is?"

Louisa shrugged, keeping a small smug smile on her lips, knowing it would infuriate Finch.

"Never mind. I'll find him on my own," Finch snapped. "But my first priority is to locate some missing property.

From the South," he added meaningfully. "You might be able to help me there."

"If I take your meaning, and being tarred with the abolitionist brush I think I do, I find the suggestion of helping you find anything, or anyone, unlikely," Louisa said, letting her distaste show plainly.

"Look, Miss Alcott, one of the things I've learned is that your whole family doesn't have two coins to rub together. If you help me, I can change that. I'll pay good money for information." He pulled out a billfold thick with currency.

Glancing back down the alley, Louisa saw Mr. Pryor come out with an empty crate. Spying Finch and Louisa, Pryor's eyes widened when he saw Finch's money. His dismay only strengthened Louisa's resolve. Pryor didn't think she was able to handle the slave catcher on her own. Well, wouldn't he be surprised.

She lowered her voice so Finch had to come closer to hear her. "Mr. Finch," Louisa began. "I would do anything to help my family. What kind of information do you need?"

He smiled. "I'll show you," he said, pulling a folded piece of paper from his billfold. Keeping it hidden from anyone passing by, he unfolded it and displayed it to Louisa. It was a wanted poster, illustrated with a drawing of a fugitive slave. She caught her breath, then forced herself to exhale normally. It would not do for Finch to realize how recognizable George's likeness was. Out of the corner of her eye, she saw Pryor still watching them.

"I don't know him," she lied. "But even if I did, why would I tell you when I could collect the whole reward? For my family's sake, of course."

His eyes narrowed, but the smile stayed on his lips. "If you read carefully, the reward is for capture." Finch kept the amount of the reward folded so Louisa couldn't see what George was worth. "This slave is dangerous and won't go back South without a fight." He casually drew back the coat to reveal a pistol stuck in his belt. Leering over Louisa, he spoke in a confiding voice that made Louisa wish for a tub of hot water, soap, and a stiff brush. "I, however, am prepared to take him by force. I just have to bring him back breathing. His condition is entirely up to him . . . and to anyone foolish enough to hide him."

Suddenly, the game Louisa was playing tasted sour in her mouth. "Mr. Finch, your occupation is vile. I know nothing about your missing slave—but if I did, I'd rather shoot you dead than give him up to you!" She tore the poster from his hands and ripped it into pieces. He grabbed at it and she pushed him away with all her might. He stumbled back a step but recovered himself easily.

Mr. Pryor came rushing forward. "Miss Alcott, are you hurt? Is this man pestering you?"

Shaking with anger, Louisa nodded. "Of course, Mr. Pryor. Mr. Finch was just telling me about his business of hunting men like animals and returning them to their owners for a life of degradation!"

Finch glared at her.

"I think you'd best leave the young lady alone," Mr. Pryor said, shooting Louisa a stern warning look.

"Stay out of this," snarled Finch. "I wouldn't be surprised if you were in on this Railroad business, too."

Pryor was a good actor and didn't flinch. Shaking his head in a puzzled fashion, he said, "Mr. . . . Finch, is it? I have no idea what you're talking about. I was just trying to spare Miss Alcott the embarrassment of a public scene."

"I don't need your protection." Louisa's words were drowned out by Finch, who said loudly, "That's very noble of you, Pryor, especially when you seem so eager to avoid public scrutiny."

Mr. Pryor's eyes narrowed and between lips drawn tight, he asked, "What do you mean?"

"I've been watching you. You own this tavern, don't you?" Finch's eyes were fixed on Pryor. "My hotel room looks out over your alley. Imagine my surprise when I saw you receiving deliveries in the middle of the night. I thought, what a dedicated businessman this tavernkeeper must be."

"When you own a business, you work all hours," Pryor muttered.

"Now, I'm in town looking for a missing slave. So I naturally wondered if there was any possibility your shipment was of the human variety. And then of course I see the daughter of an abolitionist slipping out of your alley . . . Mr. Pryor, it looks suspicious."

"You must not have looked very closely when you were spying on me last night." Pryor had given up any pretence of politeness. "I received a shipment of whiskey early this morning. The early bird gets the worm, I always say."

"I saw the whiskey, but then I asked myself another question. Do all those cases of whiskey have the proper tax stamps?"

Pryor was quiet, but his sudden stillness spoke the truth.

"If Miss Alcott will excuse us, shall we discuss it further?" Finch said.

Mutely, Pryor nodded and let Finch go ahead of him into the alley. Pryor held back for a moment and whispered for Louisa's ears only, "I told you not to talk to him!"

"I didn't have a choice," Louisa retorted. "And at least the only dangerous secrets I have are about our package. Can you say the same?" Pryor glared at her but followed Finch down the alley. Louisa wondered if Mr. Pryor was quite safe. If Finch threatened him with exposure, would Pryor keep their confidences?

Louisa started purposefully toward the general store to rejoin Marmee when a voice called her name from the porch of the new Middlesex Hotel. Reluctantly, Louisa halted and watched Miss Whittaker come down the front steps. Dodging a carriage and a farm wagon laden with straw, she made a beeline for Louisa.

Miss Whittaker was slender, with the graceful neck of a swan. Her dark hair tumbled down her back in ringlets that appeared loose but were actually carefully arranged. Her traveling dress was of a royal blue and was corseted to make her waist appear tiny. Louisa envied the rich fabric, if not the corset. She smoothed her own skirt, wishing the scorch marks from when she stood too close to the fire didn't show up so much on the pale cloth.

Louisa plastered a fake smile on her face. "Good morning, Miss Whittaker."

"Dear Louisa!" Miss Whittaker gushed. "Is it true? Your mother is leaving us?" Her arms were as outstretched as the tight sleeves of her dress allowed. Louisa imperceptibly stepped away from the possibility of any embrace. A furrow appeared between Miss Whittaker's eyebrows, then disappeared. Miss Whittaker dropped her elegant hands to her sides. "When does Mrs. Alcott leave?" she asked.

"In less than an hour," Louisa said. "She's doing some last-minute shopping. So if you'll excuse me . . ."

"Of course. And please be sure to tell her that she needn't worry about dear Mr. Alcott. I'll drop in every day to make sure he is coping without her."

"I'm perfectly capable of taking care of my father," Louisa said sharply, ignoring Miss Whittaker's lips pursing. "It's not necessary for you to bother him while he is writing."

Miss Whittaker tried another tack. "And he must write, write, write! My investors want only the best essays."

Louisa's attention sharpened at the word "investors." "Miss Whittaker, I hope you aren't expecting any financial contribution to your magazine from my father." Thank goodness Marmee wasn't here to scold Louisa for her presumption. But Marmee had left her in charge—the sooner she started, the better.

"Of course not," Miss Whittaker assured her. "His contribution is his name and reputation. And Mr. Emerson's and Mr. Thoreau's, of course. My investors are confident that they will recoup their money."

"How much have you raised?" Louisa asked.

Miss Whittaker's eyes narrowed, and she answered grudgingly. "Nearly a thousand dollars so far. Enough to fund several issues of my new magazine." She fingered one of her ringlets, almost purring with satisfaction.

"A thousand?" Louisa repeated faintly. "And how much of that will go to the writers?"

"At first, nothing. But as soon as we are established, then we will pay the writers very well indeed."

"But without their essays, you have no magazine," Louisa argued. "They should be paid from the start."

"Mr. Alcott assured me that that would not be necessary," Miss Whittaker said.

Louisa sighed. That, unfortunately, had the ring of truth.

Mr. Finch emerged from the alley alone and headed straight for Louisa. "Miss Alcott, I don't think we finished our conversation."

Miss Whittaker turned to the new arrival and Louisa was surprised to see her porcelain complexion whiten like bone.

"Won't you introduce me to your friend?" Finch said, coming face-to-face with Miss Whittaker. He stepped back in surprise. "Edith? Is that you? Edith Climpson?"

Miss Whittaker touched Louisa's arm to steady herself. "Whittaker," Miss Whittaker said hurriedly. "My name is Whittaker."

"Of course. Edith Whittaker," he said, a malicious smile on his lips. "It's been several years since I saw you last. It was in Washington, wasn't it?"

"The less said about Washington, the better," Miss Whittaker said, with a glance at Louisa.

"Of course. Whatever you like. Tell me, what are you doing here?" he asked. "Were you looking for me? I was born and raised in Concord."

"Certainly not!" cried Miss Whittaker. "I had no idea that you were from this area. I'm here on business."

Louisa watched the two of them, feeling like a spectator at a masquerade. "Business?" Mr. Finch stressed the word. "Perhaps I can be of assistance?"

"Not likely!" Miss Whittaker spat. She saw the surprise on Louisa's face and became more ladylike. "I am perfectly capable of managing my own affairs."

"Nevertheless, I'm at your service," Finch said.

"It's completely unnecessary," Miss Whittaker insisted. "Now Miss Alcott and I must escort Mrs. Alcott to the train."

Marmee, May in tow, finally emerged from the general store and looked impatiently up and down the street. Mid-morning was a busy time for the Main Street shops and at first Marmee didn't notice Louisa. Louisa whistled to draw her mother's attention, ignoring Miss Whittaker's scandalized look. Marmee turned and saw her, waving her arm for Louisa to come.

"I'm afraid we are in a dreadful hurry, Miss Whittaker," Louisa said. "I'll just leave you here with Mr. . . ." She watched Miss Whittaker, curious to know if he too had answered to a different name in Washington.

"Mr. Jones and I have nothing further to say to each other."

Mr. Finch's cheeks reddened, and he had the air of someone who could barely keep his temper in check. "Miss Whittaker," he said with some emphasis. "You're confusing me with someone else. My name is Finch."

"In Concord, I dare say it is," Miss Whittaker replied. She seemed to have recovered her equanimity.

Marmee tapped her watch impatiently, so Louisa wasted no more time and ran toward her, away from a most uncomfortable reunion.

"Where have you been, Louisa?" Marmee asked as they set off at a brisk pace toward the train station. "Who were you talking to?" Although she could still read without spectacles, Marmee's eyesight was not good for long distances. Little May skipped ahead, clutching a bag of treats.

"Miss Whittaker," Louisa answered, making a split-second decision not to worry Marmee about Mr. Finch. "She caught me on the street."

"Miss Whittaker is very fast," agreed Marmee with a wicked glint in her eyes.

With an answering grin, Louisa said, "You should see how quickly she can trap Mr. Emerson in his own study!"

"At least he tries to run. Your father surrenders willingly!"

"Marmee!" Louisa said, laughing, but disconcerted at the same time.

"None of that, young lady." Marmee waggled a finger at Louisa. "You know as well as I do that your father's fatal flaw is not a woman but the promise of publication. Miss Whittaker is tempting him with this magazine of hers."

Louisa nodded thoughtfully, and after a moment told her mother everything Miss Whittaker had said about her magazine. "Do you really believe she's raised so much money?" Louisa asked.

Marmee shrugged. "As long as we don't owe anything, I don't care. But I won't hold my breath waiting for her to pay your father. Louisa, in this world, you have to depend . . ."

"On yourself," Louisa finished. "I know, Marmee. But *you* can depend on *me*. I'll make sure Father doesn't lose his head or his purse."

The train depot was in sight now. Far in the distance, they could hear the whistle of the train to Boston. From Boston,

Marmee would take a stagecoach to New Hampshire. Louisa started to say something to her mother about the train being on time, when she realized that her mother was wrestling with some private concern. Finally she spoke. "Louisa, I don't know how to ask you this . . ."

"Just ask, Marmee. I'll do anything."

"I trust your father completely, but . . . Miss Whittaker is persistent." Marmee's back was rod straight, and a flush started at the hollow of her neck and went to her hairline.

Louisa impulsively threw her arms around her mother. "I'll make certain that Miss Whittaker's visits are always chaperoned. I won't give her the chance to compromise Father."

Marmee clutched her close, then pushed her away, keeping her hands on Louisa's shoulders and looking her straight in the eyes. "My darling Louy. I ask so much from you. I'm so proud that you're able to take on all these challenges. I only wish you didn't have to grow up so fast."

"Marmee, if I can lighten your burden, I don't mind." Louisa lifted her chin, letting Marmee's praise buoy her.

A long, plaintive whistle announced the train's arrival. The next few minutes were a blur of loading trunks, presenting tickets, and lifting May into the train. Before Marmee climbed into the train car, she pressed a note into Louisa's hand. Then Marmee said her farewells and the train puffed away. May waved from the window. A small stream of disembarking passengers headed into town on foot or in carriages.

Louisa unfolded the note. Marmee had poured all her confidence in Louisa onto the page. She suggested Louisa write
every day as a safety valve to her strong emotions. But above
all, Louisa should have faith in herself.

Alone, Louisa walked toward home. Marmee was right:
Louisa was *capable*. And it was time to show everyone, especially the ones who doubted her.

CHAPTER SEVEN

With the delightful enthusiasm of youth,
they took the solitary boy into their midst and
made much of him, and he found something very
charming in the innocent companionship of
these simple-hearted girls.

*L*ouisa took back paths home, picking her way across bogs. It would have been quicker to take the main road, but what waited for her at home except chores and responsibilities? As she walked, she thought about Marmee speeding toward adventure while Louisa had to stay at home. How was she to write interesting stories if she never went anywhere or met anyone?

She cut through Mr. Emerson's extensive orchards until she reached the Alcotts' stand of apple trees. From there she could just glimpse their house and the occasional traffic on the main road to Lexington.

Louisa heard the sound of chopping before she saw her father wielding an axe on an apple tree that had been struck dead by lightning a few months ago. She smiled, thinking how the wood would burn sweetly in the fire after it sat for a bit. Although her father refused to work for anyone else, he never shirked his duties at home. He loved farming and carpentry, welcoming the opportunity to put his theories into practice. This meant that their house was filled with unusual features, like indoor showers. On the other hand, Marmee and her daughters had to surreptitiously grow potatoes because Father mistrusted root vegetables. He preferred produce that didn't grow under the ground. Since apple trees reached for the heavens, he considered them a purer fruit.

The axe lifted high, then swung down to remove a large branch. Without a pause, the axe came up again. Another branch fell to the earth. She cocked her head, wondering at how quickly her father was working. She drew closer and saw with surprise it wasn't her father. It was George, dressed in her father's working clothes and leather gloves and even his floppy straw hat, a gift to Bronson from Henry Thoreau. Even if Finch were stupid, which he wasn't, George was just asking to be noticed.

Louisa carefully scanned the fields and relaxed ever so slightly when she didn't see any curious eyes. Quickly, she drew close and called out, "Hello, George."

He turned quickly, holding the axe with both hands across his body, ready to strike. "Miss Louisa—I'm sorry." He lowered the weapon. "I didn't hear you come up behind me."

"No, George, it is I who is sorry—I shouldn't have sneaked up on you," she reassured him. "But you can't be out here, George. It's not safe."

"I asked your father if there was anything I could do. He suggested this." He indicated a pile of branches, all grotesquely twisted and bent. Louisa realized the wood wasn't for firewood at all. "He wants them for a building project," George went on.

Louisa pushed down a surge of anger. How could her father be so stupid? Even disguised, George was working out in the open, where any passerby might notice him chopping wood on the Alcott land. "My father was mistaken. You have to go back to the barn. Now."

George opened his mouth to say something, then saw her face and remained silent. He collected the axe. Louisa said, "Wait here. I'll make sure the road is empty before you come closer." She ran to the stone wall that set off their orchard from the road and checked in both directions. There was a solitary man heading her way, but he was too far to see them clearly. They had enough time. She waved an arm, and George loped across the road to their garden and into the barn.

"You must stay hidden," she said as she opened the secret door to his hidden room.

"Anything you say, Miss Louisa," he said.

"I haven't forgotten my promise to bring you a book. I think you'll like *Robinson Crusoe*." She grinned. "What we Alcotts lack in material wealth, we make up for in books."

George hesitated, then asked, "Have you any news of my family?" He didn't try to hide his worry.

"The Conductor says four or five days. That's all I know."

He closed his eyes and his lips moved in silent prayer.

"So you must keep yourself safe until they come." Louisa paused, then continued in a whisper. "The man you warned me about—he's here. His name is Finch and he suspects us of being part of the Railroad."

"I saw a man watching your house this morning," he said. "Very early. I had gone out to . . . relieve myself . . ."

On pins and needles, Louisa asked, "Did he see you?"

He shook his head. "No, he was watching the house, not the barn. I told Mr. Alcott first thing this morning."

"He didn't think to mention it to me," Louisa said, barely containing her bitterness. Father was going to have to learn to trust her, or George might pay with his freedom. And maybe the Alcotts, too.

"If this Finch thinks you're hiding me, it's not safe for any of us." George's eyes were full of concern. "I don't want to bring trouble to your house."

"He thinks I may know something. He'll be watching me. So from now on, I will lead him on a chase away from the barn. My sister Beth will take care of your meals." Louisa placed her hand on his arm. "Rest easy; we won't give you away."

"Of course not, Miss Louisa. I have faith in you." His simple words warmed her heart as much as Marmee's had. "Besides, I've come too far to be caught now."

"But mind that you be careful. Don't show yourself." She paused. "Even if Father says it is safe."

Bidding George farewell, Louisa left the barn. Her home glowed in the afternoon sun. The hill rising behind the house was called Revolutionary Ridge, a name that conjured blood and death, but these days the hill hummed with new life and the promise of summer. The garden was filled with every shade of new green and dozens of birds flitted about the sky, carrying twigs for their nests. Even her industrious woodpecker was trying to drill a hole in the chicken coop. Louisa sympathized. She would have to work just as hard as the tireless bird to feed all the mouths in her care.

The man coming down the road from town was closer now but not so close that he could have seen George. She watched out of curiosity, wondering who he was.

He wore a dark coat and a soft felt hat and carried a suitcase and bouquet of flowers. Not a farmer, she thought, and he didn't have the air of a merchant, either. She wondered if he had arrived by the train. He walked like a young man, but he was too far away for her to distinguish his features. Louisa felt that there was something familiar about the way he moved, but she could not place the recollection.

Slowly she circled the house, keeping out of sight, to stand in the shadow of the front porch. With all the secrets going on around town these days, she told herself, it only made sense to pay close attention to strangers.

As the man reached Hillside, he stopped. She stiffened, watching him carefully. Louisa caught a glimpse of his profile. He looked a bit like Fred, a very distant cousin who often stayed summers with the Alcotts. Fred was like a brother to Louisa; he had been a dear companion who was game for any adventure, even if he couldn't always keep up with her when they ran in the woods. She hadn't seen him in almost a year, since he went away to school. Although this man resembled Fred, he was taller and broader.

The young man made his decision and unlatched the gate with a resolve that Fred could never manage. Approaching the door, he rubbed the back of his neck.

Louisa let out a sharp exhalation of recognition. Only Fred had that particular mannerism. But how he had changed since last summer!

"Fred?" Louisa stepped out from her hidden alcove, startling him. "Fred, is that you?"

He started toward her. "Louisa?"

"It *is* you!" she cried in delight. She stepped toward him, arms held out in welcome. Then she checked herself. Her friend Fred had been a companion on a hundred walks in the woods or trips on the river. She could hug *him,* but this young man in a suit felt like a stranger.

Fred had no such qualms. He dropped his case and his bouquet. "Louisa, didn't you recognize me?" he laughed. "Have I changed so much in a year?" He took her in his arms and swung her in an embrace that lifted her feet from the ground. His hat tumbled off, revealing an unmistakable head of curly red hair.

She slapped at his chest. "Put me down. When did you grow so tall that you could spin me around like a top?" Finally he let her go. "How are you here, dear Fred?" She put her hand to her bodice to catch her breath. "Marmee didn't say a word!"

"She doesn't know. I'm so busy at the university that I hardly write anyone. But I had some free time, and no one else I'd rather spend it with than the Alcotts. So I boarded a train and here I am." He grinned, revealing straight white teeth. "Now take me to the family. I cannot wait to see the expression on Marmee's face."

"But Fred, that's just it," Louisa exclaimed. "Marmee's gone! She and May just left for the entire summer for New Hampshire. And Anne is gone teaching. It's just me, Beth, and Father."

His open face fell, but then he brightened again. "Well, I'll just have to settle for you, then," he said, teasing her with his large blue eyes. How disconcerting, she thought. Fred's friendly eyes were exactly the same, but the rest of his face was much improved. How had she never noticed his perfectly straight nose?

"Come in, then," she said, laughing.

He reached down and collected the flowers and presented them to her. She shook her head with a smile. "You must give them to Beth. She'll appreciate your fine ways and little attentions."

"Still the same Louisa, I see," he teased. "Someday you have to grow up and be a young lady."

"Not until I absolutely have to," she retorted. "But Beth is plenty ladylike enough for both of us."

"Did she get the sheet music I sent her at Christmas?" he asked, following her inside.

"She did. Marmee said what a clever gift it was because it made us all merry with her piano playing. Now put down that case and sit down." She gave him a gentle shove into the parlor. "I'll fetch everyone. Won't they be surprised!"

Whirling around, she raced up the stairs, calling "Beth, Beth!" She burst into Beth's room to find her sister resting in bed. "Come down, come down quick. There's a surprise in the parlor for you! No, don't bother to fix your hair. This surprise likes you just as you are!"

Like a gust of wind, Louisa blew out of the room in search of Father. She found him in the kitchen, sitting with his elbows on the table and his chin resting on his hands. When

Louisa barged in, she stopped short at the look of misery in his eyes.

"Father!" she gasped. "Are you all right?"

He stood up suddenly, shoving the table away from him. "Of course I am. Louisa, why are you running around so wild? Haven't I told you a dozen times that if you carry yourself in a constant tempest, you will never find peace in your mind?"

"Oh, Father, not a dozen. You've told me that at least a score of times," Louisa said sourly. Their relations were always like this, she reflected. Every gesture on her part rebuffed. Every concern met with a scold. Nothing about her speech, her appearance, or her manners pleased him.

In the excitement of Fred's arrival, she had forgotten that she had a bone to pick with her father. "Father, how could you tell George to go out in the orchard?"

"The poor man was restless, cooped up in that small room. I thought some physical activity would do him good. And I needed some of that twisted wood for the door I'm designing for Emerson."

"It was foolish. There's a slave catcher after him who will stop at nothing to find him. How long do you think it would take Finch to hear about a black man chopping wood for the Alcotts?"

"The orchard is on our property, set back from the road. It was perfectly safe," Bronson defended himself. "And I don't appreciate your tone. Anyone would think you were the adult here instead of an intemperate child."

"George is my responsibility, and I'll thank you not to get him caught because of your recklessness."

"Louisa, your tone is disrespectful and—and rude," he spluttered.

"I'm speaking my mind. I thought you valued self-expression, Father," Louisa said, her words sweet with a touch of acid. "Oh, by the way, we have a visitor in the parlor." She turned on her heel and left, ignoring his querulous voice asking who it was.

In the center of the parlor Beth was wrapped in Fred's embrace, although, mindful of her delicate health, he stooped to keep her feet on the ground. When Bronson finally followed Louisa into the room, he bellowed, "Fred, old fellow, is that you returned to us at last?"

Placing Beth gently on the sofa, Fred turned and faced Bronson. Ducking his head with respect, he said, "Yes, sir. I've come back to you from university." He stuck out his hand and Bronson shook it heartily.

"I want to hear all the nonsense they've put in your head and cure you of it," Bronson said, smacking Fred on the back. "I never went to school, and I'm skeptical that they teach you anything you can't get on your own with a life of honest labor and reflection. I hope you'll stay."

Fred's ruddy face grew flushed. Glancing at Louisa, he said, "I had hoped to stay here at Hillside, but I just heard that Mrs. Alcott is away."

"So? Your company will help us bear her absence." Looking more closely at Fred's embarrassed face, Bronson said, "Don't think you'll put us out. Louisa tells me constantly what an efficient housekeeper she is. One more mouth to feed won't test her powers one bit, will it, Louisa?" he said with a malicious lift of one eyebrow.

"And I'll be glad to help," Beth called from the sofa.

"It's no trouble at all," Louisa assured him, all the while wondering how she was going to find food enough to feed the family, George, and a strapping young man like Fred.

"Then I'll stay!" Fred said. "I've saved some money to put toward my board."

Bronson began to say, "Nonsense, I won't allow it," but Louisa spoke over his words. "Why, thank you, Fred, that will be most welcome."

"Where should we put him, Father?" Beth asked.

"He can stay in Anne's room," Bronson said.

Anne's room was next to Louisa's, separated only by a thin wall. Her pulse ran quicker at the thought of Fred sleeping just a few feet away. They would be able to hear each other's movements and know the moment the other fell asleep. She gave herself a little shake. Even if he had suddenly become a handsome man, this was still old Fred. They had climbed trees together and caught frogs in the river. Their friendship was more interesting and valuable to her than any flirtation could be. She glanced up to find him watching her. For the first time, Louisa dropped her eyes first.

CHAPTER EIGHT

Disagreeable as it was to help get dinner,
it was harder still to go begging for it.

omorrow we'll have the first of the strawberries,"
Louisa promised as she laid the table for the evening meal.
"But for tonight, the pickings are slim." Even though Fred was
accustomed to their ways, Louisa felt ashamed of the plain
fare she served. Soup—again—bread, and the last of the apples
made up the entire dinner.

"Louisa!" Her father shot her a disapproving look. "Plain food strengthens the body, but too much richness weakens the mind."

"Maybe so, sir," Fred said. "But to my mind, the company is what makes a meal worth eating, and I'd choose the Alcott table over an extravagant feast with anyone else."

Bronson clapped him on the shoulder. "Well expressed, young Fred."

"Oh yes," echoed Beth faintly, her eyes fixed on Fred's face.

"Enough, or we'll all get swelled heads," Louisa grumbled. "At least the flowers are pretty." She gestured to the sideboard where a vase stood, filled with the flowers Fred had brought. Fred had presented them to Beth like a knight giving his lady a token. Louisa had to hide her smile when she saw how Beth blushed.

As they ate, Bronson expounded on the life cycle of the apple, stabbing the last fruit on his knife and using it for an example. Fred hung on every word and even Louisa had to admit that Father spoke very well. How typical it was, she thought, that her father's words could fill the room, entertain and amaze, and then fade away like frost on a sunny day. It was no wonder the Alcotts were poor, when her father's best asset was so ephemeral.

Fred amused them with stories about his time at school in New Haven. Father responded with tales of his days as a Yankee peddler. After the last plate was cleared, they adjourned to the parlor. Beth played the piano until her fingers hurt and the house rang with their singing. Even Louisa sang. Somehow when Fred joined her in a duet, she forgot to feel self-conscious about her lack of musicality.

The sun had set but the moon had not yet risen when there was a gentle tap on the front door. It was Mr. Emerson. It was the first time Louisa had seen him since she learned about Henry and Lidian. As she hung up his coat, she watched him closely, but somehow he looked exactly the same as always. If Lidian was betraying him, Mr. Emerson didn't seem to know it.

"How tactful you are to come after dinner," she murmured to him.

"Prudent, my dear," he confided. "I like a joint of meat and wine with my meal."

"You won't find those here," Louisa agreed.

Mr. Emerson was surprised but delighted to see Fred, and soon the gentlemen were seated in front of the fire, talking.

"It's good to have Fred back," Beth said to Louisa as they washed the dishes in the kitchen. "I thought we would be so sad and lonely tonight without Marmee and May."

Louisa scrubbed the dishes, splashing soapy water about the sink. "I did, too. But Fred filled up some of the empty space."

As Louisa brought tea into the parlor, Bronson was bragging to Fred about the family's connection to the Underground Railroad. Louisa frowned. She would prefer to keep their involvement secret. But what harm could come from telling Fred? He was as reliable as the sunrise. And for his part, Fred was delighted to learn that his old friends were part of the Underground Railroad and he had many questions about George.

As Bronson extolled their fugitive's virtues, Emerson stood by the mantel, fiddling with a book. He carefully straightened it out and turned to Bronson.

"My old friend, I think you should be distancing yourself from the Railroad right now. With your wife away, don't take on additional responsibilities."

Louisa rolled her eyes. As if Father was exerting himself for George! The only thing he'd done for the fugitive was put him in jeopardy.

"Waldo," Bronson answered after a brief silence. "Shouldn't we turn the question around? Why aren't you taking on this responsibility? You're the bravest man I know. I heard you give a fine speech denouncing slavery, but you won't join the Railroad?"

Emerson frowned. "Do you remember that speech? I gave it at the church and the sexton refused to ring the bell to tell people I was starting. That speech wasn't popular; Lidian and I weren't invited anywhere for weeks."

Bronson snorted. "What need do men such as we have for social respectability? Better to uphold one's principle in thought and deed than compromise for the sake of an invitation to tea!"

"What would you have me do?" Emerson asked. "Break the law and hide strangers in my root cellar?"

"Yes!" Bronson exclaimed.

Emerson shook his head. "Helping one slave at a time is tackling the matter piecemeal. Better to work to change the laws of the land rather than break them. Besides, every slave who escapes makes it harder for the ones who remain in captivity."

Louisa watched Emerson closely, trying to decide if his words were logical or simply a justification for his inaction.

"You should meet our guest. He is a noble man who deserves his freedom. He can read and reason as well as Fred here." Bronson shook his head gravely. "Waldo, we cannot take our own liberty for granted but refuse it to others."

"But you are chancing your own liberty. What happens to your family if you end up in jail? The risks . . ." Mr. Emerson began.

"Are acceptable to me," Bronson finished.

Fred, who had been listening respectfully, suddenly summoned the courage to speak, "Mr. Alcott, the risk is worth taking, and I admire you for it. But should the girls be involved? Louisa should not be endangered for your ideals."

Bronson's head jerked up and he glared at Fred from under his bushy eyebrows. Before he could take Fred to task, Louisa stepped in.

"I'm almost sixteen, Fred Llewellyn! Old enough to make up my own mind. *I* found George. He was alone, scared, and needing my help. As an abolitionist, I'm bound to come to his aid."

Bronson and Mr. Emerson exchanged amused glances while Fred stumbled over his apologies.

"You heard her, Fred," Bronson said. "She sounds just like her mother when her mind's made up." His voice flattened, as though the resemblance wasn't entirely welcome.

"How could we stand by and do nothing?" Beth chimed in, startling the others who had almost forgotten her presence.

Bronson strode over to Beth and enveloped her in his long arms. "Beth, my fine, brave girl!"

With a pang, Louisa turned away and busied herself rearranging the sheet music on Beth's small piano. Although she had the same convictions as Beth, Father never approved of her like that.

She started when a hand touched her shoulder. It was Fred. He spoke quietly, for her ears only.

"Beth is a kind soul, but I admire your courage more. You are a warrior for goodness."

She elbowed him, but not too hard. "You are an idiotic boy."

"I'm not a boy, although I'll concede the foolish part," he said laughing.

In better humor, Louisa turned back to the small group. Mr. Emerson stood up to go. "Thank you for a lovely evening, Louisa. Your mother would be proud to see you take up her mantle so well." Louisa couldn't help noticing the emphasis he put on the word "mantle." She glanced at the mantel of the fireplace and received an approving nod from Mr. Emerson. He bowed to Beth. "Bronson, Fred, good night. Louisa, bring Fred to the house: Lidian will be pleased to see him. I'm leaving for Boston early tomorrow morning, but I'll be back in a few days."

"Will you see Ellen?" Louisa asked. Ellen was his oldest daughter, and Louisa's sometime pupil. "I hope she's enjoying her visit with her cousins."

He nodded. "I'll take her your regards."

After Emerson left, Beth showed Fred his room and Bronson retired to his study. Louisa went to the mantel and opened the book there. A ten-dollar bill lay between the pages. Smiling, Louisa slipped it in her pocket. Tomorrow she would go shopping and the family would eat well. Thank goodness for Mr. Emerson.

CHAPTER NINE

It's bad enough to be a girl, anyway,
when I like boy's games and work and manners!

After the household had gone to sleep, Louisa lay in bed staring out her window. She'd heard Fred moving about the adjoining room for a few minutes but then nothing. She sighed and tossed the blankets aside and went to her desk. So much had happened today; she couldn't tamely go to sleep. Then she pushed herself away without even dipping her pen in ink. There was only one thing to be done.

She pulled on her boots, wrapped her warmest shawl about her, and stepped out into the garden. The moon was three-quarters full and cast a pure, cold light over the garden.

"Less than an hour." A voice came out of the shadows next to the house. She jumped before she realized the voice was a familiar one.

"Fred! What are you doing out here? You scared me half to death!"

"When I saw that your new room had a door to the garden, I laid a wager with myself. How long before Louisa sneaks out to explore the night? I thought you'd wait until midnight at least."

Smiling, Louisa put her fingers to her lips. Glancing at the dark house, she gestured for him to come away with her. They climbed up the hill behind the house. Bronson had terraced the path in a clever zigzag to make the climb less demanding. Halfway up the hill was a comfortable bench Bronson had built. No matter what his shortcomings were as a provider, Louisa often had reason to be grateful that her father was such a clever architect and carpenter.

Fred wiped the bench clean of dew with his handkerchief.

"How gallant," she exclaimed. "I suppose I have to curtsy to the fine gentleman now?"

"The essence of being a gentleman is that I don't notice if you do or not," Fred said haughtily, nose in the air. They both laughed and collapsed onto the bench.

"We can see the whole town," she said, gesturing with her whole arm at the panoramic view. "There's the steeple of the Congregational Church. See how it glistens in the moonlight? Oh, you can see our post office from here."

The "post office" was a tree stump at the base of the hill. Father had hollowed out a space inside the wood and built a clever door at just the right height for children to use as a post office. The Alcott girls used it as a secret place to exchange letters, poems, and books. Last summer Fred had left a small bouquet in it every morning for Marmee. Even Father had taken to leaving letters of advice to his daughters there.

"Is the old post office still going?" Fred asked.

Louisa shrugged. "Not now. With Anne and May away, there's only me and Beth." A light breeze pushed against their faces. "Look, you can see Mr. Emerson sitting in his study!"

Fred looked obediently. Without turning back to Louisa he said, "Louisa, as lovely as this view is, I don't think it's the reason you're wandering in the middle of the night."

"I had more things to think about than would fit in my little room," she admitted.

"Was I one of them?" he teased.

"Of course. But you were the least upsetting thing . . . Oh, I don't mean that. I am very happy to see you. But other things happened that require some thought."

"Tell me," he said. "Let me help."

"You know about George, but wait until you hear the rest." She told him about Mr. Finch, Miss Whittaker, and Mr. Pryor. "And in addition to all this trouble, I have the care of the whole house while Marmee is away!"

"That is an awful lot." Fred was thoughtful. "Let's see: Beth will help with the house. Together, we'll all keep George safe. And I'm here now to keep this Finch character from bothering you. That leaves the lovely Miss Whittaker. Can I meet her?"

Louisa wrinkled her nose at him. "She's just your type," she said loftily. "Artificial, well-dressed, and as polished as a mirror."

"Firstly, that's not my type at all," he said, with an amused lift of his eyebrows. "My type is a young woman with a bad temper and messy hair who is an indifferent cook."

"I knew you didn't like the soup!" Louisa said, then blushed as she realized she was suggesting that she was Fred's type.

"The soup was fine but the company was better." He held up a second finger. "Secondly, I'd like to meet Miss Whittaker so that I can describe her to a friend of mine in Washington."

Her embarrassment forgotten, Louisa clapped her hands in excitement. "So you can ask about a certain Miss Climpson whose name mysteriously changed on the journey from Washington to Concord?"

"Exactly. Her story is suspicious to me. If she was up to no good there . . ."

"Then perhaps she's up to no good here." Her sharp nod sent her long, thick hair flying. "That's a capital idea!"

Fred caught a strand of her hair, rubbing it between his fingers. "Your hair is the color of chestnuts. It's quite beautiful, even if it's all a-tangle."

Secretly pleased with the compliment, Louisa took pains not to show it. "Miss Whittaker tells me it's unfashionably long."

"It's even longer than last year."

"It's such a bother to take care of. I'm planning to chop it all off soon," Louisa promised. "The barber told me he'd give me good money for it."

"You mustn't do that," he cried. "It's your best feature." With a sly grin, he said, "Without it, you might be mistaken for a boy."

"And what's wrong with that?" Louisa cried, gathering her hair and putting it on top of her head. "Boys have it all their way in this world."

"I used to think so, too, but now I see that young ladies have more power than I thought," he said.

"If I were not a girl, then all the faults that I am most scolded for would be considered blessings," Louisa said matter-of-factly. "Father would love me if I were a son." In Fred's eyes, she saw the reflection of her forlorn expression.

He put his hand over hers. "He loves you. He just doesn't recognize that you are a lovely young woman, not a child any longer. But I do."

Louisa went very still. "Fred, don't," she began. She pulled her cloak tighter across her chest, uneasily aware that she wore only her nightgown. A year ago, she wouldn't have cared, but tonight she couldn't help but think of how inappropriate her clothing was.

"Louisa Alcott, can't you take a compliment from an old friend?"

Watching him warily, as though he might suddenly drop to one knee and propose, Louisa said in her primmest tone, "Thank you, Mr. Llewellyn."

"That's better," he said with a smile. "Now, Louisa . . ."

"Look!" she interrupted, pointing at the sky. "A shooting star."

They were silent for a few minutes, only speaking occasionally to point out a new star that had joined the twinkling tapestry in the sky. Finally Fred said, "It is beautiful up here. I wonder that you ever sleep when you can enjoy the world like this at night."

A stray memory crossed Louisa's mind, making her smile.

"What is it?" Fred asked.

Louisa tilted her head to one side. "Do you want to hear something I've never told another soul?"

Fred stretched his arm across the back of the bench and said, "Of course."

"When I was little, Mr. Emerson gave me a book to read. It was about a little girl named Bettina, who was Goethe's muse. I wanted so much to be Mr. Emerson's muse. I'd sneak out at night and leave him posies on his porch. And I would spend hours up here just watching the light in his study window."

"Did he ever know?"

"I hope not!" Louisa shook her head violently. "I wrote him dozens of letters, but luckily I thought better of sending them. And eventually I grew up and out of my infatuation." She drew her knees up on the bench and hugged them close. "But while it lasted, it was glorious."

Fred chuckled. "You are full of surprises. I'd like to see those unsent letters—I daresay they'd make for fascinating reading."

"I daresay," Louisa said, giving him a gentle shove. "But I burnt them all long ago—I'm careful with what I leave behind. I might die tomorrow, and it would be too utterly shaming for that story to outlast me."

"Only fifteen and already considering your legacy?" Fred mocked.

"Oh, I'll have one," Louisa assured him. "Someday I'm going to have a fortune of my own."

"Everyone wants to be rich. The question is how?"

Louisa pretended to consider, as if she hadn't done this mental exercise hundreds of times. "I've no one to leave it to me. I won't marry for it. That leaves earning it."

"Again, how?"

"Once I thought I might be an actress."

"You were the star of every play we put on in the barn," Fred agreed.

"But Marmee thinks it is unbecoming, so that leaves my writing. I'll get rich and famous through my novels."

"Of course. Why didn't I think of that?" Fred smacked a hand to his forehead. Louisa glared at him, unsure if he was mocking her. "Tell me, Miss Alcott, what magnificent opus are you writing now?"

"A novel about an extremely worthy girl. She's penniless. And an orphan."

"Naturally."

"Through her purity and kindness, she charms an aristocratic English family and eventually wins the heart of a rich lord."

"Hmmm," Fred said. "That's your idea of a happy ending? She marries money?"

"She marries for love, but he happens to have money. She'll be happier that way. You don't know how awful it is to be so poor, but I do."

Fred's father was a lawyer, and he had enough money to send Fred to school but not much was left over.

"So you'd never marry a poor man?" Fred's joking manner had deserted him.

"I don't think I'll ever marry," Louisa said seriously. "I couldn't give up my independence." She allowed herself to think for a moment about all that she wished to do and see, all the stories she wanted to write.

"But . . ."

Louisa put her chin in her hand, staring down at her house. "Who else but me will take care of my family? I'm doomed to be an old maid, with a pen instead of a husband, and a heap of novels in place of children."

"Now, Louisa Alcott, that would be a tragedy," Fred cried. "I'll not let it happen." He put his arms around her, bent his head to hers, and kissed her.

Louisa's mouth parted in surprise; Fred took advantage to kiss her more deeply. The bristles of his beard rubbed against her cheek, his firm lips pressed against her soft ones.

She pushed him away with such force that he fell off the end of the bench. "Fred Llewellyn, don't do that again!" she cried as she turned to flee down the hill.

"But Louisa!" Fred's words were lost in the darkness as Louisa sprinted down the hill and back into her room.

Safely inside, she shut the door and leaned against it, panting, her heart thrumming.

CHAPTER TEN

"You won't show the soft side of your character,
and if a fellow gets a peep at it by accident
and can't help showing that he likes it,
you . . . throw cold water over him, and get so
thorny no one dares touch or look at you."

$\mathcal{L}$ouisa, is everything all right?" Beth asked as they set the table for breakfast with plain wooden bowls and flax linen napkins.

"Of course," Louisa answered. But she didn't meet her sister's eye. A thick lock of hair slipped free of Louisa's hastily fixed bun.

"You look as though you haven't slept a wink and you're as skittish as Goethe." Beth deliberately slammed the milk pitcher on the table. Louisa jumped. "See," Beth crowed. "I told you so!"

"It's nothing." Louisa stirred the porridge on the stove, adding raisins as a special treat.

Beth smiled. "Those are Fred's favorite."

Louisa blushed, cursing Fred for his distracting presence in her thoughts. "Will you call Father and Fred to the table?" she said, more sharply than she intended.

"Louisa," Beth began. "I need to tell you something about Father . . ."

"Later, Beth," Louisa said sharply. "After breakfast."

Her brow uncharacteristically furrowed, Beth left without a word.

Louisa stirred as the porridge thickened. The night before, Fred had remained outside for almost an hour. Then he had knocked quietly at her door. Pressed against the door on the other side, her heart beating so loudly Louisa was sure he must hear it, she had not answered. She had touched her lips, tender from her first kiss. It was a moment she'd not even dared to dream about. But Louisa wouldn't fall in love with a poor man like Marmee had. Not for kisses, not for love, not for anything.

Finally Fred had gone to his room and she had listened to his pacing, as regular as the ticking of a clock, until she had fallen asleep. When she woke, her dreams had left faint shadows of Fred, etched just below the surface of her thoughts. Try as she might, she couldn't remember what she dreamed about.

Louisa told herself she was not listening for Fred, but when she heard his deep voice talking with Beth, her stomach leaped. What would he say to her? Would he be cross? He had no right to be; he had acted the thief and stolen a kiss from her. Perhaps he would expect her to be angry? Or contrite? Would he understand if she told him that she was more confused than anything else? Did this dizzy feeling mean she cared for Fred as more than a friend? Was love like flying on the back of a leaf in a storm?

"Ugh! I'm all discombobulated!" She threw the porridge spoon across the room, where it stuck to the wall next to the door.

"This doesn't bode well for breakfast," Fred said, filling the doorway. His thick red hair was tousled about his head and his blue eyes were bright with mischief. He had to tug hard to pull the spoon away from the plaster, then he handed it to her. "Good morning, Louisa," he said. "I hope you slept well."

She nodded, not trusting her voice to respond. His smile was charming; his crooked teeth lent his face a dash of imperfection that was appealing. She wished she could look somewhere besides his mouth, but it was impossible. She recalled every detail of his kiss and felt the warmth color her cheeks.

Beth followed Fred into the room and went to the icebox to get the milk.

"I slept well, too," Fred said. "Although I had the strangest dream of wandering out in the garden with a lovely sprite. She floated out of my reach and then disappeared altogether."

Louisa beamed. What a clever way to air the subject without any embarrassing details and in a way that naïve thirteen-year-old Beth wouldn't understand. Louisa took up the challenge. "Isn't it strange how one's imagination plays tricks on one?"

"Clearly." His eyes glistening with mischief, he said, "Because I thought my sprite was a beautiful maiden—but it turns out she was just a tomboy in disguise."

Louisa couldn't help it; she burst out laughing.

"What's so funny?" asked Beth.

"Nothing," Louisa and Fred replied simultaneously.

"Good morning." Father came in and sat down. He looked well rested, and Louisa wondered that he had spent his first night away from Marmee with so little strain. Didn't he miss her at all? With a pang of remorse, Louisa remembered how miserable he had looked before dinner the night before.

He took a spoonful of the porridge that Beth put in front of him. "Raisins? Your mother never puts raisins in the por-ridge. And so much sugar."

Louisa bristled. "We're celebrating Fred's first morning with us." She put a pitcher with cream on the table.

"*And* cream? Louisa, it's unnecessary. Fred didn't come to us for gluttonous meals."

Fred brought his bowl to be filled by Louisa and whispered in her ear, "Gluttony would be the *last* reason to come to the Alcotts'!"

With Fred at her side, Louisa felt as though her father's scolding was bearable. Father went on, "He came for reflection and high thinking. It's a waste of time dressing up plain porridge."

"Father, it's breakfast, not a philosophical conundrum," Louisa said. He glowered at her and she met his gaze defiantly. However were they to find their way to peace if they fought over porridge?

Beth began to chatter, filling the awkward silence. "Father, what will you do today?"

"I'll till the lettuce beds and then I must work on Emerson's gazebo."

Louisa noticed Beth shoot her father a puzzled look, a crinkle appearing above her fair eyebrows.

"Emerson's gazebo?" Fred asked.

"Mr. Emerson liked Father's gazebo so much he asked Father to build one on his property, too. I think he's getting more than he bargained for," Louisa explained. "Father calls it the Sylvan, but Mrs. Emerson calls it the Ruin."

"Mrs. Emerson doesn't understand Father's architectural ideas," Beth hurried to say.

"I'd like to see it," Fred said.

With a mischievous grin, Louisa said, "The townspeople visit regularly and wager on when it will collapse."

Bronson stroked his chin. "I think they'll be surprised."

"Louy, what are you doing today?" Beth asked.

"Housework and more housework." Louisa began ticking her chores off on her fingers. "I must clean up the breakfast dishes, dust the parlor, beat the rugs, and set the bread to rising and the peas to soaking." On any other day, she wouldn't mind the chores so much. The work was only for her hands, not for her mind. She used her housekeeping time to dream. But today an adventure with Fred beckoned.

Fred said plaintively, "That will take forever, Louisa! I thought we could go for a long walk as we used to."

"We don't have any servants; it all takes time," Louisa answered. "And *then* I have to go convince the store to give us more food on credit, and . . ." She stopped suddenly, aware too late of her father's stormy look.

Her father shoved his chair out from the table and stood up abruptly. "Your mother managed this house and all of you without the need to bore us with the tedious details. It is unfortunate she didn't teach you the same." He stalked out of the room, leaving Louisa red-faced and furious.

Once again, Beth's chatter filled the silence. "Louy, I'll help with the chores so you and Fred can get out sooner."

"I'll help, too," Fred said. "So we have time to find Henry Thoreau if we can."

"I don't know where Henry is," Louisa said, squeezing Beth's hand in gratitude. "With Finch looking for him, I think Henry made himself scarce rather than lead him to our 'package.'" Henry had avoided her, she thought, ever since she had learned about his feelings for Lidian.

"I've often thought about him while I was away," Fred said. "He told me once that an early morning walk is a blessing for the whole day."

"And so do you walk every morning?" Louisa asked, cheering up.

He turned up his palms and shrugged. "No, but I think about it while I lie abed!"

Everyone laughed. Louisa laughed loudest, mostly from relief. Fred's stolen kiss wasn't going to ruin the easy give-and-take of their friendship.

"What are you doing, Beth?" she asked. "I think you should plan to rest today."

Beth shook her head. "I want to pick lots and lots of strawberries." She held up a finger to stop Louisa's protest. "And *then* I'll lie down and do some sewing. I'm making a shirt and a set of handkerchiefs for George. He'll need them when he's free."

"That sounds restful. And I'm sure George will be eternally grateful," Fred said. "What is it your father calls you? Little Tranquillity? As for Louisa, she's . . ."

"A hurricane! And don't you forget it!" Louisa said, handing him the breakfast bowls.

He followed her to the sink. "What *can* I do to help the Misses Alcott?" Fred asked.

Beth and Louisa exchanged glances and said in a single voice, "The rugs!"

While Louisa finished up in the kitchen, Fred manhandled the bulky carpets out of the house and into the garden. Beth brought him a broom to beat them clean. When he returned, he was dusty but the rugs were not. Fred mopped his perspiring face with a handkerchief supplied by the helpful Beth.

While Fred tidied himself up, Louisa tucked her long hair up in a net. Beth watched from her customary spot on the sofa. Watching Beth in the mirror's reflection, Louisa asked in her most casual voice, "Beth, why did you seem surprised by Father's plans for the day? It sounds like any other day."

Beth caught her lower lip between her teeth, looking anywhere but at her sister. It was very unlike her, thought Louisa. "Beth! You can tell me."

"This morning I was brushing Father's coat—the one he wore yesterday. This fell out of the pocket." Beth reached into her sewing basket and pulled out a visiting card. "It's Miss Whittaker's. And on the back she wrote only 'Tomorrow. The gazebo. One o'clock.'"

"Oh my," Louisa said, her mind working frantically. What would Marmee want her to do? "I'm sure it's just about Miss Whittaker's new magazine." Although Louisa didn't entirely believe this, she didn't want to worry Beth.

"Louy, I don't like Miss Whittaker. And I wish Father didn't seem to enjoy her company so much." Beth hesitated, and then with her cheeks pink with embarrassment, she added, "Especially with Marmee away."

"I don't care for her, either," Louisa said. "But Father adores Marmee and would never do anything to hurt her."

Beth raised a hand to her lips. "Oh, I know, it's terrible of me to even suggest such a thing!"

Louisa rushed to the couch and knelt at Beth's side. "But you aren't suggesting anything about Father—it's Miss Whittaker you don't trust. And neither do I."

"What should we do?" Beth asked, her voice almost a wail.

"Darling, don't worry," Louisa said, giving her a quick hug. "Fred and I will stop by the gazebo at the appointed time. Any tête-à-tête that Miss Whittaker has planned with Father will quickly become a quartet!"

*   *   *

One of Louisa's last tasks was to assemble a midday meal for George. She asked if Fred would like to meet George. He agreed eagerly.

"Check the road and garden," she told Fred as she stuffed a paper sack with apples, bread, and a jug of apple cider.

"What am I looking for?" he asked as he obediently went to the garden door.

"Anyone who is too curious about us. But especially a big man with fair hair. That's Finch."

Fred soon returned and said, "There's no sign of anyone there who shouldn't be." He looked at the sack. "Are those his provisions?"

Louisa nodded. "These are to feed his body. But I think he's dreadfully bored." She went into the parlor, examining the bookshelves. Fred followed, holding the sack. "Ah, here it is."

"*Robinson Crusoe*?" Fred asked. "So it's true that George can read and write?"

Louisa nodded. "He's very intelligent. I'm not surprised his former owner wants him back so badly." She tucked the book in with the food. "Let's go."

They quickly crossed the road and entered the barn. Louisa went to the corner and knocked once, paused, then knocked three more times.

"There's a secret room here?" Fred asked. "We've spent hours here doing your theatricals and playing games and you never let on?"

"Father and Marmee never even told me!" Louisa assured him. "Not until they decided I was old enough to help with the Railroad."

The door opened just wide enough for them to enter.

"Good morning, George," Louisa said cheerfully as she slipped through the doorway. "Did you sleep well?"

"To tell the truth, Miss, I don't sleep well at all," George said. Even though there was plenty of room to stand up straight, he stooped, as though confinement was shrinking him. "I worry that every noise I hear is that slave catcher come to take me back." He caught sight of Fred and looked expectantly at Louisa.

"George Freedman, this is our dear friend Fred Llewellyn. He's like a member of the family. I wanted you to meet him so you would know you could trust him if something goes wrong."

Fred stepped forward and held out his hand. "Mr. Freedman, it's an honor to meet you."

George took the outstretched hand, and seemed to stand a little taller. "No, I am honored, Mr. Llewellyn, sir."

"I've got to feed the chickens and collect the eggs," Louisa said. "Fred, why don't you and George talk a little and I'll come back and fetch you."

"If Mr. Freedman will permit me to stay, I would enjoy that," Fred said very formally. His courtesy was a compliment to George and Louisa was proud of him. She left them alone to become better acquainted.

As she emerged from the henhouse, the last chore complete, Fred was waiting for her. He was full of praise for George.

"I know. He's very sweet," Louisa agreed. "I'll put these eggs inside and then we can go."

"Finally!"

Before they set out on their ramble, Fred wanted to put on his hat, but Louisa dissuaded him. She preferred his head bare. To match, she pulled off her hair net and shoved it in her pocket. As they walked, Fred complained to Louisa for setting such a quick pace.

"Your stamina has declined at college," she teased. "I'm not walking any faster than I have in the past."

"I think you are trying to stay ahead of me so I cannot kiss you again."

Louisa laughed. "Don't be silly."

His face lit up. "So you *do* want me to kiss you again?"

In an arch voice that she barely recognized, Louisa said, "Not in broad daylight, sir. Think of my reputation!"

"As if you cared what anyone thought!" Fred laughed. But he seemed content with the half-promise in her words.

Louisa slowed her pace and they walked together, their steps evenly matched.

"Do you remember that time you put on the pirate play in the barn?" Fred asked.

"Of course. I wrote it, didn't I?" Louisa said.

"And played most of the parts as well," he laughed. "It would have been useful to have known about that secret room. We could have used it for the costume changes."

"Do you remember how the first time I performed it I had to wear my plain shoes?" Louisa tugged her skirt up to reveal a pair of much-mended laced leather shoes. "And I said that I would only perform the play a second time if I had proper pirate boots! And a few days later I went to the post office, and jammed into our little box was a pair of the most excellent pirate footwear I'd ever seen." She looked at Fred with a speculative air. "No one ever admitted to giving me those boots."

"I really wanted to see the play again," Fred said. "So I went into Boston and found you a pair of seaman's boots."

"I still have them and write at least one character in every play to wear them."

"Watching you be a pirate is one of the reasons I came home," Fred said. "You are utterly adorable."

"That's the most foolish thing you've ever said," Louisa said. "And that's saying a lot."

CHAPTER ELEVEN

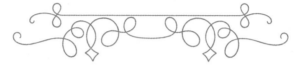

But her reverence for genius received
a severe shock that night,
and it took her some time to recover
from the discovery that
the great creatures were only men and
women after all.

After walking for a few minutes, Fred said, "I'd for-gotten that Walden Pond was so far."

"Far? It's only two miles. You have gotten lazy."

Two years ago, Walden Pond had been a favorite haunt of theirs. They often went to catch tadpoles, search for arrow-heads, or, best of all, visit Henry in his little cabin. Henry had lived there for almost two years until he felt that he had achieved his goal of living simply and close to nature. Louisa's favorite memory of that time was sitting with Henry in a canoe on the pond while he charmed the birds out of the trees with his flute. Now that he was back living at his mother's house on the other side of town, he still returned to the cabin when he had serious thinking to do or essays to write.

The most direct path to Walden Pond led through a walnut grove on Mr. Emerson's land. In fact, Henry's cabin was built on Mr. Emerson's property. Louisa wished for the hundredth time that Henry would stay far away from Lidian Emerson.

Fred picked up a nut and broke it open. It was rotten.

"They were better in the fall," Louisa said. "Mr. Emerson let us pick as many as we wanted."

Fred tossed the nut aside. Not looking at Louisa directly, he asked, "Is it really true that Mr. Emerson doesn't support the abolitionists?"

Louisa hopped over a log lying across the path. "He does, just not the way we expect." She told Fred about the money left in the book the night before. "When he supports us, he's supporting the cause. But I don't think he wants to do so publicly yet. He has a reputation, and his speaking engagements are the family's main income. He's not like Father or Henry, who wouldn't mind being arrested in the least."

"They'd use their imprisonment to advocate for the cause," Fred agreed. "All the fellows at school were green with envy that I knew the great Mr. Emerson. But still, I find it disappointing that he doesn't want to get his hands dirty."

"So do I. But I can be patient."

"You?" Fred burst out laughing.

"Someday Mr. Emerson will be as fully committed we are. He's too good a man to avoid the field of battle forever."

Their conversation died down as they walked along a narrow creek. Suddenly, Fred slowed at a small stand of wild crocus. He bent down and picked a bunch, presenting it with a small bow to Louisa. "Amends for my behavior last night, Miss Alcott."

Louisa reached to accept the bouquet, but he suddenly lifted it high above her head. "Fred!"

He grasped her hand and put it next to his heart. "It's also a declaration of my intentions," he proclaimed.

"Then give me my flowers!" Louisa said. He relented and handed them over. She admired the small flowers and tucked them into her pocket. "I'll accept your amends," she said. "As for your intentions, we'll see." She set off at a fast clip, leaving him behind.

"I hope I don't have to wait for long," Fred said as he hurried to catch up. "I'd like to kiss you again."

Louisa turned and punched him in the arm. "Fred Llewellyn, why did you want to kiss me at all?"

"Ow!" He rubbed his arm. "Because you looked very lovely in the moonlight and I couldn't help myself."

"I have so many problems to deal with right now," Louisa said. "You couldn't have chosen a worse time."

"In this life, you have to seize the moment," he said. "You must know how much I admire you. I've thought of nothing but you while I was at school. Why not give me a chance?"

"I'm not ready . . . to think about this right now," she said, trying to make him understand. "We're such good friends and it would change everything."

He stopped her on the path and put both hands on her shoulders. "Darling Louisa. I know how much you hate change. Unlike you, I really can be patient." He drew her close to him and she was perfectly still, acutely aware of his body pressing against hers. Louisa hoped he would kiss her again, all the while trying to think of how to keep him from doing it.

He leaned forward and delivered a chaste kiss on the top of her head. He turned and walked rapidly away. She stood in the middle of the path, confused and, if she were honest with herself, a little disappointed.

He looked over his shoulder. "Don't dawdle, Louisa," he teased. "The day is wasting away!"

With a growl, Louisa broke into a run and soon overtook him, her boots carrying her easily over branches and around stones. In a few minutes they arrived at the path that went round about Walden Pond. As they went around the northern end of the pond, Louisa heard a cracking noise behind them.

She put her hand on Fred's arm and stopped dead. "Did you hear that?" she asked.

Fred looked puzzled. "I didn't hear anything."

"It was like someone stepped on a branch." She turned in a circle, senses open to every sound. "It's gone now."

"You took Henry's lessons in woodcraft too seriously," Fred said. "Next we'll track an Indian by his footprints and his evening meal by the marking on his arrowheads." He began walking again and Louisa followed reluctantly.

"We've moved beyond finding arrowheads to excavating the past," she informed Fred in a lofty voice. Louisa pointed to a space that had once been a clearing but was now overgrown. "If you look carefully you can see the foundations of a little house. Henry showed me last fall. Freed slaves lived here fifty years ago."

"What happened to them?" Fred asked.

"He doesn't know." Louisa shrugged. "But he's trying to find out. I think he wants to write about them."

"Is he still planning on turning his time here into an essay?" Fred asked.

Picking her way over a muddy patch in the trail, Louisa said, "I think so. He showed me a draft of the beginning not too long ago. It was inspiring." She closed her eyes to visualize every word in his beautiful flowing handwriting. "'I went to the woods because I wished to live deliberately, to front only the essential facts of life, and see if I could not learn what it had to teach, and not, when I came to die, discover that I had not lived.'"

"You remember all that? Word for word?" Fred asked, amazed.

"How else would I remember it?" Louisa asked, lifting her eyebrows. "His ideas changed how I looked at life." She threw her arms out wide. "I couldn't bear to get to the end and realize I'd wasted my time on this earth."

"You should go to university," Fred said. "You'd think and write circles around most of the fellows at Yale."

"As if the university would allow a woman in! And even if they did, there's no money," Louisa said bitterly. "You see how we live. Debts everywhere and surviving on the charity of our friends." She shot him an angry look. First Fred proffered her love that she didn't want, then dangled in front of her nose an education she could never have. Didn't he understand that Louisa's dreams were already overfull of unattainable things?

Fred frowned, his lip twisted. "It makes me burn to see how you live in such poverty while your father refuses to work. Is he indifferent to your family's suffering? I admire him tremendously, but this aspect of his character I do not understand."

She swallowed hard but couldn't rid herself from an onslaught of angry tears. "I wish I knew. He's not averse to taking money that other people have earned, like my uncle or Mr.

Emerson. Or even Marmee! He just won't work for anyone other than himself," Louisa said, swiping furiously at her eyes. "But our situation is more desperate than anyone knows. We owe money everywhere: the general store, the stationers, even the doctor. Thankfully Dr. Bartlett won't abandon Beth's care, but we have owed him his fee for months. It's so mortifying."

"I wish there was something I could do," Fred said.

"Marmee and Anne are working," Louisa mused on as if Fred hadn't spoken. "I should, too, but jobs are scarce in Concord. Although Henry did offer me a job at his family's pencil factory."

The look of scandalized horror on Fred's face restored her sense of humor. "All right, not Henry's factory," she said.

"If only I was rich and could swoop in and solve all your family's problems!" Fred exclaimed.

"It's not your responsibility, it's mine," Louisa said, but tempered her words with a quick smile. Of all her reasons to avoid Fred's love, this was probably the truest one. Only a rich man could solve the family's financial woes, and Fred was not rich. But Louisa could never bring herself to marry for money. So, unless she happened to fall in love with a wealthy man, and even more unlikely he fell in love with her, the family's problems were hers to solve. "Don't worry. I'll think of something."

Through the trees, she caught a glimpse of the tiny rustic cabin. "There it is."

It stood in its own clearing, not far from the pond. It had only one room, with a single door, two windows, and a fireplace. The furnishings were equally spare: a narrow cot, a table, and two chairs. Henry had built it himself with help from Bronson. During Henry's self-imposed exile to Walden Pond, he had welcomed visitors, and Louisa had been inside it many times. Thoreau's little house was easily one of her favorite places.

"I don't see him," Louisa said.

"Maybe he's inside?" Fred suggested.

"On such a beautiful day?" They reached the door. As Fred lifted his hand to knock, Louisa realized that there were voices inside. Henry had company, and with a sinking feeling in her stomach she feared she knew who it was.

"Wait . . ." she said. But it was too late. Fred's fist connected with the door.

The voices stopped.

"Let's go," Louisa said, tugging on Fred's arm.

"But I thought I heard him inside," Fred said. He raised his voice. "Henry! Henry Thoreau! It's Fred Llewellyn and Louisa Alcott."

"I wish you hadn't done that," Louisa said. The door opened slowly. Henry appeared in the doorway. He wore his usual brown corduroys and a jacket of woodland green with large pockets to hold all the forest treasures he might find. The only thing that was not customary was the furious expression on his face.

"What are you doing here?" Henry asked in a clipped voice she had never heard from him before.

There was nowhere for a guest to hide in the single room. Lidian Emerson stood next to the window, looking out over the pond. Her face was scarlet and she fingered the buttons on her bodice, perhaps from nerves, or, Louisa thought with a flash of cynicism which dismayed her, Lidian might be checking to make sure the buttons were refastened correctly.

"Henry!" Fred said with delight. He stepped forward, then caught sight of Lidian. He flushed and stopped in his tracks. "Mrs. Emerson, I didn't expect . . ." he said. He ran his finger around his collar as though it had suddenly grown too tight. "How nice to see you."

"Fred. Louisa," Henry said in a clipped tone, looking at Louisa. "You weren't invited here."

As though his words had physical force, Louisa stumbled back a step. "We've never needed an invitation before."

"You aren't a child anymore," Henry snapped. "You can't just come unannounced. I have company."

"I can see that." Louisa's eyes narrowed. "As you said, I'm not a child."

Henry's face turned red. "You should go."

"I say, Henry . . ." Fred began.

"Fred, not now," Louisa said. "We're not welcome here. Goodbye, Henry, Mrs. Emerson." She turned on her heel and, grabbing Fred's hand, stalked away back into the woods, Fred on her heels, putting as much distance between them and Henry Thoreau as she could.

A man leaned against a tree in the narrow clearing, waiting for them. "We have to stop meeting like this, Miss Alcott."

Louisa stopped in surprise. "Finch," she said.

Fred started as he recognized the name. Louisa glanced behind her. The bend in the path obscured the view to Henry's cabin; for the moment Henry and Lidian were out of sight.

"What are you doing here?" Louisa asked.

Finch wore a satisfied grin on his face. "Following you."

"That is contemptible."

"So is harboring a slave." Finch paused. "Indeed, it's illegal. So you'd best tell me what you know . . ."

Louisa cut him off. "I don't know anything about a fugitive," Louisa said. "And if I did, I'd not help you for any amount of money."

"Perhaps not knowingly," Finch conceded. "But watching where you go can be very instructive." With a smirking look at Fred, Finch continued, "And with whom."

Fred stepped forward, fists clenched. "I'll thank you to leave the lady alone."

"The lady can speak for herself," Finch said.

"Yes, I can." Louisa put her hand on Fred's arm. "Fred, please don't. Fighting will only make the situation worse. I won't have you soiling your hands on him." Finch was the kind of man who fought dirty and often; he'd pulverize poor Fred in a fight.

"Every time I find a lead to my missing property," Finch said, "I find you in the middle of it. I saw a servant from the

Emerson house bring over a sack of clothes to your house. Why, I wonder? And then I hear about a negro chopping wood yesterday in your orchard. Did your family suddenly find the money to hire a field hand?"

Louisa felt a shiver down her spine, but she kept her face still.

Finch went on, "And now I find you going off to a remote part of the woods. It's just a matter of time before you lead me to him."

Louisa was relieved and scared at the same time. At least she was nowhere near George. But just around the bend were Lidian Emerson and Henry Thoreau. Finch seemed to attract scandal like a magnet did iron filings, and she didn't want to hand him any more ammunition to use against her friends.

Perhaps there was an innocent explanation about Henry and Lidian being alone in that cabin, but Finch wouldn't look for it. As furious as she was with Henry—how dare he scold her when he was the one behaving badly?—the last thing any of them needed was for Finch to catch Henry in a compromising situation with his best friend's wife.

"Mr. Finch, your informant was mistaken," Louisa said. "My father often wears black gloves and has a dark hand-kerchief wrapped around his face when he chops wood. He suffers from asthma."

"Why don't we go ask him about it together?" Finch said. "I wonder if he'll tell the same story. And I wouldn't mind taking a closer look at your barn and the outbuildings in your garden."

Louisa schooled herself not to give away any hint that Finch's guesses were hitting their target. She stared Finch down, not blinking. "We could," she said. "But my father isn't at home. We were just going to join him on the other side of Walden Pond. There's a hill there with an excellent vista. Why don't you join us?"

At her side, Fred shot her a surprised glance, but then he understood her plan was to lead Finch in the opposite direction from George's hiding place and away from Henry's cabin, too. "Louisa, we're supposed to meet him in just a few minutes," he said helpfully. "We should go."

"Not so fast, Miss Alcott." Finch was scanning the woods as he spoke. "I can't help but wonder what you were doing on this side of the pond. I remember when I was a boy there were freed slaves living in these woods. Isn't it more likely that you are out here checking on my fugitive than you are having a picnic with your father? My man is close, I'm sure of it." He watched her face closely to see if she reacted. Louisa kept a look of polite incomprehension on her face, but Fred couldn't control himself.

"George's not *your* man," Fred burst out. "Slavery is an abomination, and you're the lowest sort of scum to be hunting fugitives."

"Fred, don't . . ." Louisa snapped, but Finch was too quick for her. Eyeing Fred with speculation, Finch slowly grinned.

"Ah, so you've confirmed my man is here in Concord."

"I did no such thing!"

"Yes, you did," Finch said. "Otherwise how would you know his name? But don't feel badly; I was sure that my quarry was here anyway. And who might you be?"

"Fred Llewellyn. A friend and admirer of the Alcotts'. I warn you they are under my protection."

Finch burst into raucous laughter. "Is that so?"

"Yes. So leave them alone or you'll have me to deal with." Fred put his fists up. Louisa winced; she wished Fred wasn't such a chivalrous fool.

"And what, pray tell, my scrawny young friend, do you intend to do about it?"

Fred lunged forward, aiming a punch at Finch's nose. Finch saw Fred's move coming and ducked. Fred landed only a glancing blow, his momentum taking him past Finch, who shoved Fred's back to push him into the undergrowth. Fred sprawled amidst the ferns, his face in the dirt.

Finch held his hand toward Louisa. "Shall we explore these woods together, Miss Alcott?"

Louisa glared at him. "Never!" Turning her back on the slave catcher, she helped Fred to his feet.

"Never is a long time, Miss Alcott," Finch said.

CHAPTER TWELVE

*"The sharp words fly out before I know what
I'm about, and the more I say the worse I get,
till it's a pleasure to hurt people's feelings and say
dreadful things."*

Fred scrambled to his feet, breathing furiously through his nose. His face was smudged with dirt, and a bit of dark fern stuck up from his full head of hair. He looked ridiculous, and what was worse, he knew it. Louisa knew in her heart this was a humiliation that would stay with him.

"Miss Alcott, put your dog on a leash! He has terrible manners," Finch said, his hands smoothing his slicked-back hair. "Stay out of my business, boy."

Fred started forward, but Louisa grabbed hold of his shirt and pulled him back. "Stop, Fred. You're making things worse."

Fred stepped back, holding up his hands to show Louisa he had regained control of himself. Relieved, she turned to Finch. "Do you want to speak to my father or not?"

Finch shook his head. "You seem a bit too eager for me to leave. I'll keep looking around here."

Pretending it didn't matter, Louisa said, "Please yourself. Let's go, Fred." Before they could start walking, there was the sound of earnest conversation on the path behind them. Louisa's heart sank. Henry and Lidian, hand in hand, were talking intently and hadn't noticed them.

Lidian saw Louisa first and with a quick movement, she took back her hand. Henry spied Louisa and stopped short, eyes darting, searching for a way to escape.

Louisa jerked her head, trying futilely to warn Henry about Finch. Before her message could be understood, Finch stepped forward, blocking the path. When Henry saw Finch his face went pale.

"Finch," Henry said grudgingly, as though the name tasted bitter to his tongue.

"You've been hard to find, Thoreau," Finch replied. "I thought it was because you were harboring a fugitive slave . . ." His eyes lit upon Lidian, whose blush spoke volumes. "But now I see it was something else entirely. Won't you introduce me to your friend?" His tone was oily and made Louisa feel as though a thousand insects were crawling over her skin. Lidian's eyes were wide and frightened.

"Her name is none of your business," Henry said. "What are you doing here?" He looked at Louisa with such hostility she took a step back. "Did you bring him here?"

"Of course not!" Louisa said, her face pinking. "This loathsome man is looking for a slave and followed me." She turned to Finch. "You're welcome to search the length and breadth of Walden Pond. You won't find anything. Or anyone."

"The slave can wait," Finch said, watching Lidian. "I want to become reacquainted with my old schoolmate. And his lovely companion."

Lidian placed her hand on Henry's arm. "Henry, who is this?"

"Never mind him, Lidian," he said, his eyes darting from her to Louisa to Finch and back again.

Finch's tiny eyes widened a fraction. "Lidian Emerson? There can't be two beautiful women in town with that name."

Lidian's gasp was as good as a confession. "I can't . . . Henry, don't let him . . . I have to go!" She broke off and pushed her way past Henry and Fred. Giving Finch a wide berth, she ran away, stumbling over obstacles on the path. Henry's eyes followed her, and Louisa's heart ached at the pain in his face.

Finch watched too until Lidian was out of sight, then slowly turned back to Henry. "Shame on you, Henry. Isn't her husband your best friend? I could have warned him that you would try to take what was his. You've done it before."

Henry started forward, his fist cocked back to strike Finch.

"Henry, don't," Louisa said quietly. "He's armed."

Finch drew back his coat to reveal his pistol tucked in his belt.

Henry's eyes rested on the pistol and his hands fell to his side. "Is that what this is all about?" Henry said. "You're still angry that a woman preferred me fifteen years ago? Abigail's married to another now and has five children." As if he hadn't a care in the world, he sat on a large boulder and pulled out a small block of wood and his knife. He began to whittle. For an instant, despite all the tension in the present, Louisa was transported to her childhood, watching Henry make marvelous animals out of wood.

"You weren't even interested in her, Henry, but that didn't stop you from charming her with your strange ideas." For the briefest moment, Louisa caught a glimpse of a suffering that drove Finch to want to hurt others, and she felt a pang of sympathy. "I can see now that Abigail wasn't nearly pretty enough for you. Lidian Emerson is quite the catch—even if she's married to someone else." Finch's gleeful spite made any sympathy Louisa had for him disappear like a drop of water on a hot frying pan. "I've always wanted to meet Mr. Emerson. I'll have to stop by and introduce myself."

"As you wish," Henry said. "A meeting with Ralph Waldo Emerson cannot help but be uplifting. Especially to a man in your profession. But you're out of luck in Concord; you won't find any fugitive slaves here."

Louisa appreciated Henry's purpose, but she wished he wouldn't use George to distract Finch.

"Oh, I'll find him," Finch promised. "Despite you and your friends. But there's no reason I can't enjoy myself in the process."

Henry stared down his long Roman nose, examining Finch with his quiet blue-gray eyes as though Finch was a hitherto unknown bit of flora. A poisonous plant, Louisa thought.

"Finch, what will it take for you to go away and leave us in peace?" Henry asked quietly.

"Henry, you can't give in to the scoundrel," Fred said, his face filled with anger. "We should trounce the fellow here and now."

"Fred, please be quiet," Louisa entreated, not taking her eyes from Henry's face.

"Tell me where the slave is," Finch said. "Then perhaps I'll leave town without visiting Mr. Emerson."

"Henry, no," Louisa protested in a whisper that faded into the air.

"Even if your slave was here, none of us would tell you a thing," Henry said. "How much is the bounty? Perhaps we could make it worth your while to abandon your search and leave Concord?"

"Henry, that's extortion!" Fred exclaimed.

Henry held up his hand to silence Fred, all the while watching Finch's face closely.

Finch chuckled. "Unless you are a great deal richer than I remember, you can't afford to pay me off. I'm due a fifteen-hundred-dollar reward for this slave."

Louisa drew a quick breath. Her father had purchased their house and twelve acres of farmland for not much more than that. None of them had that kind of money, except, she acknowledged, conscious of the irony, Mr. Emerson. The one person they could not ask for help.

Finch kept talking. "I'll get what I came for. And before I leave, I'll ruin you."

Henry stood perfectly still, but his busy hands carved an animal's shape out of his block of wood.

Finch turned to Louisa. "Don't think I've forgotten your family, either. I'll see you all in jail for abetting the theft of property before I'm finished."

Louisa sucked in her breath. Next to her, Fred was only just keeping himself in check. Amused by their response to his threats, Finch smiled as he pulled out his watch. "It's later than I thought. I've an appointment in town I must attend to. But I will return."

Finch turned and walked away. Louisa sank down on a log at the side of the path and put her head in her hands. Fred stood next to her, shifting from one foot to the other. Henry stared down at the ground.

After a few minutes of silence, Louisa looked up and asked, "Henry, what are we going to do?" There was no reaction. Fred put his hand on Henry's shoulder.

A small tremor went through Henry's body and his attention returned to Louisa and Fred. He put the knife in his pocket.

"You'll do nothing, Louisa, do you hear?" Henry said. "Nothing."

"But . . ." Louisa began to protest.

"You've done enough," Henry said bitterly, his callused fingers pinching the bridge of his nose.

"Me?" Louisa could barely get the word out.

"Louisa, I know you didn't do it deliberately," Henry went on, "but nonetheless you led Finch here. You've wrecked everything. He'll destroy Lidian."

"Henry, you're not being fair!" Fred said. "Louisa tried to lead him away from you and Mrs. Emerson. She was protecting you!"

"I don't need protecting. Especially from you." Henry let his head fall back, his eyes closed.

"You blame *me*?" Louisa spat the question. "*You* have compromised yourself and Lidian. *You* have humiliated Mr. Emerson. All the fault is on your shoulders, Henry Thoreau. There's hardly any left for me."

Henry stared at her as if he had never seen her before. Perhaps he hadn't noticed that Louisa was no longer a hero-worshipping child, but a woman with her own opinions. After a moment of staring at her, he gave a little nod. "Louisa," he said, "I beg your pardon. What I said was unforgivable and you are right to take me to task for it." He turned and began to walk away.

"Henry!" Louisa called, taking a few steps after him. Fred hung back. "Where are you going?"

"To my cabin. I have some serious thinking to do."

"But what should we do about Finch?"

"Louisa, your job is to protect George. Keep Finch away from Hillside. Don't let my problems interfere with your duty."

"But what will you do?" Louisa asked.

"Whatever I have to," Henry said. "But you can depend on me not to betray you or George."

"I know that," Louisa said, trying to convince herself as well as him that she had confidence in him. She was sure of Henry's inherent decency and kindness, but lately she questioned his good judgment.

As Henry trudged away, Fred took her arm. Wiping his brow, his eyes met Louisa's and he smiled ruefully. "And I thought Concord was a dull little town," he said.

CHAPTER THIRTEEN

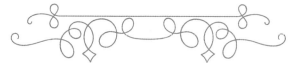

I'm neat and cool and comfortable,
quite proper for a dusty walk on a warm day.
If people care more for my clothes than they do
for me, I don't wish to see them.

"What do we do now?" Fred asked as he and Louisa retraced their steps toward home.

Louisa didn't answer, too preoccupied to reply.

After a moment, Fred said, "Louisa, what *are* we going to do about Finch?"

Louisa stopped without warning in the middle of the path and Fred swerved to avoid running into her. He opened his mouth to complain but shut it again. Louisa's eyes were fixed on an imaginary horizon, her brows pulled together and her mouth working as though she was having a serious conversation with herself. Fred had seen her in this state before. It was where her mind went when she was inventing her stories or had a serious puzzle to solve. She called it her vortex.

"The problem is, we have too many problems," she pronounced finally. "Fred? Fred?" Her eyes darted up and down the path and found him sitting on a boulder about twenty feet away.

"Oh, you're back?" he said with a teasing grin.

Louisa put her hands on her hips. "Yes. As I was saying, we have too many problems. But Finch is at the center of most of them. He has to go!"

Fred lifted an eyebrow. "Will you shoot him or should I?" Louisa gave him a sharp look. The edge to his joking words reminded her of the humiliation Fred had suffered at Finch's fists.

"Why is Finch in Concord?" Louisa asked rhetorically.

"Well . . ."

"Because his fugitive slave is here," Louisa finished triumphantly. "If George left, then Finch would follow him. All the spite in the world wouldn't weigh more with him than that fat reward."

"But Louisa," Fred said gently. "George has nowhere to go. That's why he's in your barn."

"I have to talk to Mr. Pryor." She glanced around the forest path to be sure they were alone. "He's the Conductor," she said in a hushed voice. "It's his decision if George has to change hiding places."

"You said he had problems with Finch, too," Fred said. "I'd think Pryor would want to lead him as far away and astray as possible."

"Exactly." With a sharp nod, Louisa started walking. Over her shoulder she said, "I'll need your help; you have to go to the tavern."

"If you insist," Fred said with a grin.

"Finch already suspects Pryor's involvement in the Railroad, and he'd be sure if he saw me go there. But he won't pay any attention to you," Louisa said.

"Because he doesn't think I'm a threat," Fred said sourly.

"He's wrong, Fred, but I for one am grateful if he underestimates you. I'll wander by the shops and generally make myself obvious while you tell Mr. Pryor what I propose. Hopefully if Finch is watching, he'll watch me, not you."

Fred nodded. "It's a good idea, even if it depends on Finch thinking me a fool. Do you still want to go home or go straight to town?"

Louisa glanced up at the sun. "What time is it?"

Fred pulled out his watch. "Half past twelve o'clock."

"Let's just make sure that Beth is all right." Her forehead crinkled in worry.

"What's wrong?" Fred asked.

She shrugged. "I just want to be sure that Beth is home and George is still well hidden."

When they arrived at Hillside, Beth wasn't there.

Fred pointed to Beth's sewing basket abandoned on the sofa. "Didn't she say she was going to be sewing all day?" Fred asked, fingering the handkerchiefs in the basket.

"She might have gone out visiting or to the shops," Louisa said, anxious but trying not to show it. She checked the rack where their shawls were hung. "Her shawl is gone." Growing more concerned, Louisa sent Fred to check on George.

He came hurrying back. "George isn't there, either," Fred said. "Perhaps they're together?"

"Why would they be?" Louisa snapped. "George is a fugitive and Beth is so delicate. They should both be home and safe."

She looked around the empty parlor, reflecting on how rare it was that no one was in the house. Any other time she might enjoy some time to talk with Fred alone, but today she had too many worries to think about herself. "Let's not get diverted from our plan. First things first. You go talk to Mr. Pryor and I'll look for Beth."

Fred held the door open for her. As she hurried through to the garden, she added, "And Fred, if we see Finch, then I suggest we turn the tables on him."

"How?"

"I'm tired of not knowing when he's going to show up and make mischief. This time we'll follow him instead of the other way around."

*   *   *

By the time they had walked to the Wright Tavern it was one o'clock. Louisa peeked in the window. The tavern was filled with men, mostly clerks and farmers eating the main meal of the day, but Pryor was nowhere to be seen. "He must be in there somewhere," she said.

Fred lifted her chin up and gazed at her steadily. "You look exhausted. Let's meet in the hotel restaurant in twenty minutes or so and have a cup of tea."

For a moment, Louisa let herself enjoy his soft hands, a scholar's hands, on her skin. "I have no money to spend on tea," Louisa reminded him. But her stomach growled. It had been a long time since breakfast.

"I have enough." He gave her a gentle push in the direction of the hotel. "Now go."

Louisa first visited the grocer, the bookbinder, and the stationer's shop. No one had seen Beth, and she had to fight down a rising sense of panic. She was ready to cross the street and visit the baker when she saw Miss Whittaker climbing the wide steps to the porch of the Middlesex Hotel. Louisa followed close on her heels.

The hotel was brand-new, rebuilt after the old one had burned down the year before. This was the first time Louisa had gone inside. She hurried past the long oaken counter where guests checked in and some uncomfortable-looking armchairs that were scattered about the lobby.

"Oh, Miss Whittaker!" Louisa called.

Miss Whittaker froze, then turned slowly. Her wary expression faded when she saw Louisa, leaving only disdain. "Miss Alcott," she said in a flat voice.

Louisa blinked at her appearance. Miss Whittaker's toilette was normally impeccable, but her pale skirt was marred by green stains flecked with spots of red. Long tresses of hair had escaped her perfect hairdressing and her forehead had a sheen of perspiration.

"Have you seen Beth?" Louisa asked urgently.

Miss Whittaker frowned. "Who on earth is Beth?"

"My sister," Louisa said, pushing down her irritation. "You've met her several times."

"I can't be expected to remember all the Alcott brats."

"No, you are only interested in my father," Louisa countered. "Weren't you supposed to spend the afternoon discussing business with him?"

"We no longer have any business to discuss," Miss Whittaker said flatly. "I've decided to abandon my magazine project."

"Really?" Louisa's eyebrows lifted. "Just yesterday you spoke as if it was well under way."

"Circumstances have changed," Miss Whittaker said.

"Does my father know?" Louisa asked.

"Of course he does. Now, good day, Miss Alcott. I'm going to my room now."

Disliking Miss Whittaker more than ever, Louisa's curiosity drove her to ask, "Are you feeling well?"

"Of course, why wouldn't I be?" Miss Whittaker snapped.

"You always look so elegant; it's quite a shock to see you so . . . untidy."

"I've had an upsetting day and now I want to lie down," Miss Whittaker said. "I trust you'll excuse me." Lifting her skirts, she practically ran up the stairs.

Her mind working frantically, Louisa watched Miss Whittaker disappear. Louisa would wager all her pocket money that Finch was involved in Miss Whittaker's change of plans.

She touched her fingers to her dry lips, realizing how parched she was. Fred's idea was a good one, even if it was extravagant. She headed for the small restaurant in the hotel where a waiter in a black suit blocked her way.

"I'd like some tea," Louisa said.

His eye traveled from her messy hair to her dirty boots. Louisa looked down as well. Her dress was soiled with grass stains and dirt. She quickly piled her thick chestnut hair back into her hair net, dusted the skirt futilely, and stomped her boots to get rid of any mud. Louisa turned back to the waiter. "I'd like some tea," she repeated.

"Follow me, Miss," the waiter said, his face pinched and dis-approving. He seated Louisa in a dark corner near the kitchen.

As she waited to be served, Louisa tried to sort out all the puzzles and problems. Where could Beth be? Why was Fred taking so long? What if Pryor didn't believe that Fred was trustworthy? Why was Miss Whittaker behaving so peculiarly? Where was George? And lastly, where was a waitress with her tea?

When a waitress finally appeared, wearing a cap and apron, her pale green eyes and blond hair, combined with her thin frame, chimed a chord in Louisa's memory.

"Miss Alcott?" the girl said. "I don't suppose you remember me?"

"Judith?" Louisa asked, mercifully recalling the girl's name. Judith's family had fallen on hard times a few years ago. Despite the Alcotts' perpetual poverty, Marmee had still managed to organize food and clothing for the children in Judith's family and Louisa had been drafted to deliver the supplies. Judith was only a year or two younger than Louisa. "How are you?"

"I'm very well, thank you," Judith answered. "And my Pa is healthy again. When we say our prayers at night, we always include your family, especially your Ma."

A wave of wanting her mother swamped Louisa, but she managed to say, "Thank you."

"What can I get for you?" Judith asked.

"Tea for myself and for my friend, who will be joining me in a moment."

"Would you like some cakes or scones?"

"No, thank you." Her stomach made a rumbling noise, and at first Louisa was mortified, then both girls started to giggle. "I'd love to, but I'm economizing."

"Of course, Miss Alcott," Judith said tactfully. She started to turn away.

Louisa placed a hand on Judith's wrist. "By the way, Judith, do you know Miss Whittaker? She's a guest at the hotel."

"Of course; we all know her. She gives a lot of trouble and never says so much as a thank you afterward," Judith said. Suddenly, her eyes widened as she realized she might have been indiscreet. "Miss, is she a friend of yours?"

"Not at all. She's just an acquaintance of my father's," Louisa hurried to reassure her. "So like you, I have to be polite to her. What do you know about her?"

With a conspiratorial smile, Judith answered, "Not much, except that the manager is about to throw her out of the hotel."

"She hasn't paid her bill?" Louisa guessed.

"No, much worse! She had a gentleman in her room."

Louisa lifted her eyebrows. "Really?"

Judith shook her head with an air of knowing more about the world than her age would suggest. "The manager keeps an eye on female guests, especially those traveling alone. He tries to mind his own business, but he couldn't ignore the screaming match in her room late last night. The other guests complained." She leaned in. "The Middlesex isn't that kind of hotel."

"Who was she arguing with?" Louisa asked, sliding to the edge of her seat to hear better.

"I don't know his name, but he's not a guest."

"What did this gentleman look like?" Louisa asked, trying to keep away the worry that it could have been her father. After Mr. Emerson left the night before, Bronson could easily have slipped out to visit Miss Whittaker.

The manager of the restaurant beckoned to Judith. "I have to go," she said. Before she hurried away, she whispered, "I've heard he's been asking questions everywhere. Tall and fair. Speaks like a Southerner."

Louisa exhaled in relief. Not Father but Finch.

A few minutes later Judith returned with a steaming pot of tea, two china cups and saucers, and a plate of scones.

"But I didn't order . . ." Louisa began.

Judith winked. "They're my treat. Without your family, mine might have starved."

Marmee was always saying to cast your bread upon the waters. Apparently it floated back as pastries. Nibbling on one, Louisa thanked her. "By any chance, did you happen to hear what Miss Whittaker and her friend were arguing about?"

"I didn't," Judith said. Louisa sat back, disappointed. Judith scanned the room to make sure that the manager's attention was elsewhere. "But my friend Sally was helping one of the guests get to bed in the room next door. She heard bits and pieces."

Louisa's hand trembled a little as she poured herself a cup of tea. "And what did she hear?"

"I don't hold with gossip, Miss Alcott," Judith said.

"Of course not," Louisa said. "But I assure you I have a good reason for asking."

"Yes, *you* do."

Louisa tilted her head, wondering why Judith was so emphatic.

Judith hurried on, "Sally told me that they were arguing about money. Miss Whittaker had some sort of scheme that involved Mr. Alcott. And Mr. Emerson, too. The man threatened to tell Mr. Alcott everything if she didn't give him half the money."

"Did Sally happen to overhear what this scheme was?"

Judith shook her head.

"Well, never mind," Louisa said. "If you hear anything else, please let me know." She paused. "Since it's about my family."

"Of course, Miss Alcott."

The moment Judith turned away, Fred came hurrying in. "Well?" she asked. "What did Pryor say?"

Fred poured some tea and took a sip, but the liquid was still too hot. Blowing across the top of his cup, he said, "Pryor wasn't there."

"What do you mean?" Louisa asked. "It's dinnertime. It must be the busiest time of day for him."

"That's what I thought." Fred shoved a bit of scone in his mouth. Talking around the pastry, he said, "I spoke with one of the waitresses. She said without him there, they were short-handed. She was annoyed."

"Why wouldn't he be there?" Louisa wondered.

"There's more," Fred said. He put his elbows on the table and leaned forward. "Finch was there at noon."

"His appointment in town," said Louisa. "It was at the tavern?"

Fred nodded. "Finch and Pryor talked privately in Pryor's little office in the back. The waitress heard raised voices but couldn't make out any words. A few minutes after Finch left, Pryor rushed out without even telling his staff where he was going or when he would be back."

Louisa nibbled on the last bit of scone, her mind working furiously. "Pryor's missing. George isn't where he's supposed to be. I don't like those two events coinciding."

"They might not be related at all," Fred pointed out.

"But if they are . . . it doesn't look good for George," Louisa said worriedly. "Maybe Finch blackmailed Pryor into giving up George's location?"

"You told me that Pryor is"—Fred dropped his voice to barely more than a whisper—"a Conductor. That means he's trusted. I can't believe the Railroad could make such a mistake in judgment."

"Did you hear anything about Beth?" Louisa asked.

"No, but don't worry about her. Beth doesn't have anything to do with the Railroad. She's probably visiting a friend." There was silence while Louisa stirred some sugar into her tea. The Alcotts rarely had fine white sugar like this, and despite her worries she couldn't help but enjoy it thoroughly.

"And now I have something to tell you, too," Louisa said as she sipped her delightfully sweet tea. Then she related everything she'd learned from Miss Whittaker and Judith. "Whatever Finch did drove a wedge between Miss Whittaker and my father. I never thought I would be grateful to the wretched man."

"So, what do we do now?" Fred waved to Judith for the check. He opened his wallet and took a bill to cover the tea and a little bit to thank Judith. Louisa couldn't help but compare Fred's thin wallet to Finch's thick one. Why was it that the good men always seemed to be poor while the wicked ones prospered?

"I think we need to find Father right away," Louisa finally decided. "He may know where George and Beth are. And I want to ask him about his dealings with Miss Whittaker. There's something odd there." With a sharp nod, she pushed her chair back from the table. Before Fred could do likewise, Judith came hurrying up.

"Miss Alcott, I thought you should know. Miss Whittaker just sent a note down to the front desk. She's checking out!"

"When?"

"Tomorrow morning. And she asked about the first train to Boston."

"She's running," Louisa said.

CHAPTER
FOURTEEN

*"You are sixteen now, quite old enough to be
my confidant, and my experience will be useful
to you by-and-by, perhaps, in your own affairs
of this sort."*

*L*ouisa's fears had spread to Fred like a contagion and he kept pace with her as she led the way out of town along the main road.

"Where is this gazebo?" Fred asked.

"It's in that stand of pine trees past the orchards between the Lexington Road and the Cambridge Turnpike," Louisa said over her shoulder. "Father's been working on it for months.

It's quite beautiful in its way, but strange. I don't think anyone understands it. Much like Father's writing."

Fred made an impatient sound. "Louisa—you should be more tolerant of your father. He truly is a great mind."

"You say that because you don't have to suffer for his greatness," Louisa said with a sniff. "The stories I could tell you of Marmee having to beg for credit, or the sheriff coming by with a writ because we haven't paid our debts. It's the worst feeling in the world to be so poor. And Father won't do anything about it."

Fred was silent, and Louisa knew he was torn between his admiration for Bronson Alcott and his affection for the family. Nothing further was said until they neared the Emersons' front gate.

Louisa put a finger to her lips. "Shhh," she whispered. "The last person I want to see right now is Lidian Emerson, so let's be as silent as cats and just sneak by." They were almost past the house when they heard the sound of Lidian's and Mr. Emerson's second-floor bedroom window being opened. Lidian stuck her head out.

"Louisa!" Lidian called, only just loud enough to be heard. "I need to speak with you."

Louisa cursed freely under her breath. Fred started to laugh but pretended to cough instead.

"Lidian, may I come back later?" Louisa called. "I have to speak to Father."

"It's important. Please?" Lidian pleaded.

"All right," Louisa said with a sigh. "We'll come in by the kitchen."

"No, I'll meet you at the front door. I don't want the maid to see you," Lidian hissed. "And just you. I cannot speak freely in front of Fred." She spared a quick glance down to Fred. "I beg your pardon."

"Not at all, Mrs. Emerson," Fred said. Turning to Louisa he said quietly, "I'll just go ahead and find your father. Maybe Beth is with him."

"I hope so," Louisa muttered.

Fred squeezed her hand. "Now you have me worried, too. There are too many dangerous currents swirling around us today, and I don't want anyone I care about to drown."

Her throat tightening at the thought of anything happening to Beth, Louisa said, "Fred . . ."

"I promise, I won't let anything bad happen to Beth or your father. Or you." He let go of her hand.

Louisa watched him leave, wishing his words could reassure her. Wishing she were anywhere but here, Louisa went to the formal front door. Before she could knock, the door swung open and Lidian pulled her inside, shutting the front door behind them with a furtive air.

"This is silly," Louisa protested. "I come here all the time. No one would think anything of it."

Her mouth in a straight grim line, Lidian said nothing as she led Louisa to the room that served both as a formal dining room and Lidian's parlor. The room was as unlike Emerson's study as it was possible to be. While his study was ceiling-to-floor books and heavy mahogany furniture, this room was painted a soft green and had plush armchairs and small tables convenient for a lady to rest her needlepoint on. It was comfortable, but Louisa preferred Emerson's sanctum.

Indicating that Louisa should take one of the armchairs, Lidian sat down. Louisa let the uncomfortable silence linger until she couldn't bear waiting another minute.

"Lidian, you asked to speak to me. When do you plan to start?" The impertinent words slipped out, Louisa wishing she could take them back. Lidian Emerson had been nothing but kind to Louisa and her family. But Louisa couldn't help but think it was Lidian's own foolishness that was making a difficult situation even worse.

"I wanted to explain . . ." Lidian began. "About Mr. Thoreau . . ." Her face was scarlet and she fingered the ring on her left hand.

"You don't owe me any explanations," Louisa said, not hiding the weariness in her voice. "I already know more than I like."

"I don't want you to get the wrong idea. The situation is not what you might think," Lidian said. She abruptly stood up and began moving around the room. "What am I saying? You're only a child!"

"I'm almost sixteen," Louisa said. She knew exactly why Lidian was telling her this. Lidian had been living with a secret and through no fault of her own, Louisa was now privy to it. Lidian was dying to talk about Henry.

Lidian went to the window and stared out into the garden. "Henry planted those roses for me years ago, not long after we first met. Have you ever heard the story? He wrote me a poem, wrapped it with a bunch of tulips, and threw it at the window."

Louisa shifted uneasily in her seat. The last thing she wanted to hear was a charming anecdote about the start of Henry and Lidian's relationship.

"I brought the poem to Waldo. He invited Henry in. And then they became such good friends. Waldo laughed that Henry worshipped me, but he didn't take it seriously. Waldo thought of Henry as *his* friend, *his* protégé."

"You can't blame Mr. Emerson for being Henry's mentor!" Louisa blurted out.

"Do you know how difficult it is to be married to a great man?" Lidian asked sadly. "He wants a companion to talk to. But although my mind is good, it's not quite good enough to follow all of his ideas. The distance between us has grown wider every year."

"I'm sure he doesn't expect you to keep pace with his work," Louisa said, thinking that if she were married to a man like Mr. Emerson, she would be happy to learn at his feet.

"You Alcotts are all so clever. My husband would rather talk to any of you than me." Lidian's tone was sharp, as though this grievance had festered for too long.

"I don't think Mr. Emerson wants you to be a philosopher." Louisa was thoughtful. "He's proud of how good a mother you are and how well you keep his house."

"That is all I am to him: a wife and a housekeeper," Lidian burst out. "In pursuit of his giant intellect, my husband thought nothing of leaving me to go to Europe for a year. And then he had Henry move into the house while he was away! Only a husband who doesn't think of me as a woman would do that." The tears brimming in Lidian's eyes spilled onto her cheeks.

"He was concerned for your safety," Louisa pointed out. "And he trusted you." She started to stand up. She had no patience with Lidian's self-pity. It wasn't enough that she had won a man like Ralph Waldo Emerson; she had to chase Henry Thoreau, too?

"I mean no offense, Louisa—but you are an inexperienced child." Lidian reached out and took Louisa's hands and squeezed them tight. "You can't possibly understand. Your parents are still passionately in love with each other, despite all their troubles. But do you know how Waldo describes our marriage? 'A sober joy.'"

Nothing romantic there, Louisa thought. "Perhaps that's what marriage is. Building a life together and sticking to each other through the best and worst of times," Louisa argued, pulling her hands away. "How could you think of leaving Mr. Emerson?"

"Leave him?" Lidian was taken aback. "I'd never do that. I'd be a pariah. And in any case, I don't want to." She stood up and went to the fireplace, toying with the figurines she kept on the mantel. "I found solace in Henry's company. He looked at me and didn't see the mother of his children or the perfect helpmeet. It was like being half frozen and finding a warm fire." She sank into her chair and stared miserably at the floor. "But I was never unfaithful to my marriage vows. And I would never leave my husband."

"So you are just toying with Henry's feelings?" Louisa asked in a faint voice.

"No—he knows I'd never leave Waldo or the children. But he loves me anyway. I've been trying to end our friendship, but it's so hard to give up. And then this awful man Finch arrived and he misunderstood what he saw . . ." Her voice trailed away.

The silence played out as Louisa studied Lidian, wondering if she was speaking the truth. And if she was, did it matter? Finch could still wreck Lidian's life. Louisa had believed the worst—everyone else would, too.

In the distance, there was a loud bang and Lidian started, knocking over a little china shepherdess.

"I hate those hunters. Waldo is always trying to ban them from our woods, but they don't listen," she said, her hand on her bodice as if to soothe her heart. Louisa paid no attention as she considered her response to all Lidian had said.

"It's not my place to judge," Louisa said slowly. "But I do wish you and Henry had been more discreet. This man Finch hates Henry and he will think nothing of telling Mr. Emerson your secret."

"That's what I'm afraid of," Lidian said. "After I saw you in the woods, I came home and went to my room to lie down. I heard a knock at the door, but I had already instructed Maisie that I wasn't at home if anyone called." She dug into her pocket and pulled out a visiting card. "Later, I found this on the table in the hallway."

Louisa held out her hand, feeling like a teacher and Lidian an erring student who had brought some contraband to school. The white card had the name RUSSELL ALEXANDER FINCH embossed on one side.

"Did he ask for you?" Louisa asked.

Dashing the tears from her cheeks, Lidian shook her head. "He asked for Waldo! Thank goodness he's visiting the girls in Boston. But Finch means to ruin me, I just know it."

Louisa hesitated, then took Lidian's hand. "We won't let him. You've done nothing wrong."

"I said I hadn't dishonored my marriage, but in my heart I was half in love with another man. Perhaps I deserve to suffer."

"No one deserves the likes of Finch," Louisa said. "Certainly not you and Henry."

"And what about Henry?" Lidian cried. "I'm so afraid that he'll do something rash. He is so chivalrous, he might resort to violence. I'd never forgive myself if he did."

"Henry is a man of peace," Louisa protested. How could Lidian, who claimed to love him, not know that?

Lidian buried her face in her hands and said in a muffled voice, "I hope so—but there is so much at stake."

"Fred and I will help you if we can," Louisa promised.

Lidian began to protest. "I don't want Fred to know about this."

Louisa held up her hand. "Fred was there today. He already knows."

Lidian wrung her hands together.

"You can trust him; he's a gentleman. And he deeply admires Mr. Emerson and Henry." Louisa stood up and smoothed her skirt with the palms of her hands. "We're working on a plan to get Finch to leave town."

Lidian had also stood. She ran her hands over her hair, tucking away the stray bits that had escaped in her distress. Suddenly, she was restored to the Lidian Emerson that Louisa had always known, the unflappable housekeeper and well-respected wife to the great philosopher. "Thank you for your help."

"Have courage, Lidian. But now I have to find Father." Louisa quickly left the parlor, eager to be in the fresh air, away from Lidian.

Just as she left the Emersons' garden it began to rain. It was a heavy shower, the kind of rain that farmers love to see in spring. Louisa considered turning back. But almost as soon as it had started, the rain dissipated, leaving her hair dripping and her skirt heavy with water.

Halfway to the gazebo she heard the sound of someone charging through the woods, pushing branches aside and tripping over rocks. It was Fred. When she saw his ashen face she cried out, "Fred! What's wrong?" A series of terrible possibilities ran through her mind. "Is it Beth? Is Father all right?"

Fred finally reached her, breathing hard. His eyes looked haunted.

"Fred," she cried. "Tell me what happened."

"It's Finch," he said, still gasping for air. "He's . . . Louisa, brace yourself. He's dead!"

CHAPTER
FIFTEEN

"Mercy on us! What has happened?" cried Jo,
staring about her in dismay.

*L*ouisa stood, frozen, her mind trying to absorb Fred's
meaning.

"Louisa, didn't you hear me?" Fred cried, trying to catch
his breath. "Finch is dead and your father is hurt."

"Father?" Louisa's attention came into sharp focus.
"Where? What happened?"

"The gazebo. Wait, Louisa, you mustn't go. It's not seemly.
You get the doctor and I'll . . ."

"Get the doctor yourself," Louisa said before Fred could finish his sentence. Then she was running, faster than she had ever run before. She hurtled into the clearing in front of the Emersons' gazebo, then stopped short as though she had run into an invisible wall.

Finch was lying on his back on the ground. He was perfectly, unnaturally still. His arms were spread out and a crimson stain spilled across his white shirt. A few feet away, her father was pushing himself up from the ground to his knees, one hand cradling the back of his head. Blood seeped through his fingers.

"Father!" Louisa cried, hurrying to him. "Let me see." She peeled his hand away from his skull. A bump, swollen and bloody, nestled in his gray hair, which glistened with raindrops. "Can you stand?"

With Louisa's help, Bronson got to his feet. She was tall and sturdy, but she almost buckled under his weight. She helped him to a bench to one side of the gazebo's door. "Sit down. No, not there, it's wet. This spot is dry." He sank to the bench and leaned back.

"Father, what happened?"

"I don't know. I was working on the door." His hand made a half-gesture to a door he was building for the gazebo. It was unlike any other door in Concord, possibly in all of Massachusetts. Made of twisted boughs of wood from the forest and assembled in a fanciful sculpture, it was a more suitable entrance for fairies than philosophers. "Someone hit me from behind. That's all I remember."

"You didn't see Finch?" Louisa asked.

"Finch? That slave catcher you are so afraid of? Is that who he is . . . was?" Both of them avoided glancing at the body in the center of the clearing.

Louisa nodded. "Who shot him?"

"I've no idea."

"You were alone?"

He looked her straight in the eyes. "Yes, I've been alone all day." Louisa watched him carefully. She might not be as clever as her mother at spotting his evasions, but she was almost certain her father was lying.

He went on. "When I recovered my senses, I saw that man dead on the ground. Then you arrived." He moaned at the pain in his head. "Now you know everything, so stop haranguing me, Louisa."

Louisa slipped inside the gazebo and found her father's metal canteen hanging on its hook on the wall. "Drink, Father." He gratefully sipped the water.

As she stood up, he asked, "What are you going to do?" He was being unusually meek, a condition Louisa attributed to the bump on his head.

"I'm going to make sure that Finch is really dead," she said. "You sit and rest." Opening his mouth to protest, he thought better of it and closed his eyes and let her get on with the grisly task. She slowly approached Finch's body, hesitating, ready to draw back. She had never seen a man dead by violence before.

Finch's eyes were wide open, blue orbs staring blankly at the sky. His mouth was twisted in a grimace of surprise and anger. Gritting her teeth, Louisa placed her finger against his wrist. The skin was still warm to the touch but no blood pulsed through his veins.

With a sick feeling in her stomach, she examined the wound in his chest. A hole surrounded by black scorching, oozing blood. Then she remembered how she had heard a gunshot. She quickly searched the clearing, but didn't find a gun.

She returned to her father. "Father," she said gently, kneeling at his feet. He opened one eye, wincing at the light. "Where's the gun?"

"Louisa, I told you. I don't know anything about him or how he was killed. It all must have happened while I was unconscious." His voice rose an octave, and she regretted asking him anything while he was in this state.

"All right, Father, sit still." She patted his leg in reassurance. "Fred is bringing the doctor. And the sheriff."

Standing up, she put her hands on her hips and forced herself to consider the situation dispassionately. Her father's story was implausible to say the least. It was one thing to lie to his daughter, but what would the sheriff think? There was a dead body to account for; tough questions would be asked.

To protect her father from himself, she had better find the answers first.

She returned to Finch's body to look closely at his torso, keeping her eyes averted from the bullet hole. His pockets were turned inside out. There was no wallet. Louisa clearly remembered Finch's wallet, thick with bills. Maybe this was a simple robbery gone terribly awry? She pulled away his coat, gently, from his body. Finch's pistol was gone. Very few people in Concord carried weapons. Finch was most likely shot with his own gun and then the killer took it with him.

Or her? The memory of Miss Whittaker's agitation was fresh in Louisa's mind. Had Miss Whittaker been here? And if she had shot Finch, where was the pistol? Miss Whittaker's corseted gown couldn't have concealed a gun, and she had not been carrying a purse when Louisa saw her at the hotel.

Was there anything else Finch's body could tell her? She had to work quickly. Once the authorities arrived, they wouldn't welcome her interference. Louisa felt the fabric of his coat. It was damp. Now that she was looking, Finch's face was wet, too. That was from the brief rain shower. She lifted his shoulder just enough that she could touch his coat underneath the body. It was dry. So Finch was probably already dead when it had rained; otherwise his coat would be wet front and back.

Would the same logic work for Father? She went to him. "Father?"

"Yes," he said.

She was relieved that he seemed more lucid. Under the guise of offering him another drink, she managed to examine his coat. His front was dry while the back was wet.

She cast her mind back to how she had first seen her father. He had been getting to his feet. If his story was true and he was struck from behind, then he would have fallen forward. Yes, she could see a smear of dirt on his forehead. When it rained, he had been lying facedown on the ground. That surely gave credence to his story that he was unconscious when Finch was killed—otherwise who struck him down? It was more important than ever to find the missing pistol.

She circled the clearing again. Still no pistol, but there was a pile of bizarrely shaped boughs from apple trees at the north end of the clearing, the side closest to Hillside. She wondered if they were from the pile that George had been assembling at the Alcotts' orchard not too far from here.

How did they get here? The path in that direction went directly to Hillside. Had George been here? Father might have countermanded her orders that George stay hidden. She turned to ask him, but one glance at her father's pale face and she reconsidered.

She went into the gazebo. It resembled a temple from some ancient time. Made entirely of wood found in the area, it might have sprung up out of the landscape like Jack's beanstalk. There were nine entrances, each representing a Muse. Inside there were no square corners and the roof seemed to dip in the center; no one dared ask Bronson if it was deliberate. The whimsical door was the final accent to the fantastical design.

There was nothing inside except a few strawberry hulls on the ground. New strawberries. How did they get here? Did Beth bring them? But in what? Louisa didn't see a basket.

She could hear voices approaching and she knew she was out of time. Louisa returned to her father's bench. "Father, the sheriff is here," she said.

Her father was groggy but opened his eyes. His pupils were dilated, and she worried that the blow to his head had done serious damage. She hoped that Fred had brought a doctor, too.

"Father, you mustn't say anything, all right? You don't remember anything."

With a semblance of his usual authority, he said, "Louisa, I told you. I *don't* remember anything."

"Good. That's your story and you must not stray from it."

He stared at her with slightly unfocused eyes.

"Father, let me be blunt . . ."

"Are you capable of speaking any other way?" His words had a nasty edge to them.

"If you insist," Louisa said, steeling herself to be brutally honest. "Your story is improbable to say the least. If you are telling the truth . . ."

"If!" He drew himself up, wincing.

She held up a hand to silence him, all the while listening and gauging how far away the sheriff and doctor were. "Even if your story is true, no one will believe it. So when asked, say you don't remember. In the meantime, I'll try to figure out what happened."

"Louisa, you're being presumptuous and bossy. Just like your mother."

Tears sprang to Louisa's eyes. What she wouldn't give for Marmee to be here at this moment.

"I forbid you to get involved." Her father went on, "It's your job to take care of the house, not pry into murders."

"Father, you may soon find yourself grateful for my inquisitive mind."

Fred arrived at the edge of the clearing. His face was flushed and anxious. He jerked his head behind him. A moment later, the sheriff and his deputy appeared.

Sam Staples, the local sheriff, tax collector, and jailer, was a dark-haired man of medium height. He was well liked in town. His reputation for fairness reassured Louisa. He would not judge anyone without considering all the evidence.

At the moment, he was staring at the corpse in the center of the clearing. His deputy, James Beckett, an older, dull-looking man who also worked as the town blacksmith, hung back waiting for orders. Trailing both of them was a tall older man wearing a black suit that hung on his rangy frame.

"Dr. Bartlett!" Louisa cried out. "My father has been injured. He requires your attention." The doctor started for Bronson.

Sheriff Staples knelt by the body. Looking up, he said in his laconic way, "There's no hurry to see this one, Doc. The only attention he needs is from an undertaker."

CHAPTER SIXTEEN

A slight incident gave Jo the clue to the mystery,
she thought,
and lively fancy, loving heart did the rest.

The sheriff's approach to the scene of the crime was very methodical. First Dr. Bartlett examined Bronson Alcott's head. Once Dr. Bartlett said Bronson was fit enough to talk, Sheriff Staples asked some basic questions. Bronson stuck faithfully to his story. He had been alone. He remembered nothing. He had never even met Mr. Finch. Then Bronson closed his eyes and appeared to fall asleep.

"Sheriff, I think you should stop now. He needs to rest," Dr. Bartlett warned.

The deputy folded his arms and stared at Bronson with deep-rooted suspicion. Louisa thought ruefully that her father's eccentricities had left him vulnerable. The deputy would believe Bronson was capable of anything.

Stroking his chin, the sheriff walked the perimeter of the clearing. Like Louisa, he didn't find a gun. He poked inside the gazebo, keeping a close eye on the sagging roof as though he expected it to fall in on him. He came out and began interrogating Louisa and Fred.

"Mr. Llewellyn, you're a visitor?" he asked.

Fred nodded. "I'm an old friend of the Alcotts'. I'm staying with them."

"And why did you come up here today?"

Fred hesitated, glancing at Louisa. She shook her head almost imperceptibly; the sheriff didn't need to know why Fred was looking for Bronson. "I wanted to see the gazebo." He waved toward the strange structure that had sprung full-blown from Bronson's imagination.

"And what did you see when you arrived?"

"Mr. Finch was lying there dead. That was shocking enough, but then I saw Mr. Alcott on the ground, unconscious."

"Did you hear a shot?"

"I think I did," Fred said. "But I didn't think anything of it. You often hear shots in the woods."

"Where were you when you heard it?"

"On the path coming from the Emersons'."

"Was this before or after the rain?"

Louisa's estimation of the sheriff went up.

Fred considered. "It was before the rain." Louisa lost her train of thought as she watched Fred unconsciously stroke his wet curls.

"And did you see anyone else?" the sheriff asked. "Anyone lurking about the scene or running away?"

"No. I was distressed about Mr. Alcott." Fred held out his hands in apology. "I wouldn't have noticed a marching regiment."

"Are you acquainted with the dead gentleman?"

Fred's eyes rested on the body. "I met him only this morning. His name is Finch."

Louisa remembered something. "I have his card," she said, pulling it from her pocket and handing it to the sheriff.

"Russell Alexander Finch," he read. Then glancing at Fred, he asked, "And where did you meet him?"

"Miss Alcott and I met him while we were out walking near Walden Pond."

The deputy spoke for the first time. "What time was that?"

"A little before noon, I think," Fred answered, glancing at Louisa for confirmation. "He said he had an appointment in town and he left."

"And you didn't see him again?"

"Not until I found him like this." Fred pointed at Finch's still body.

"So what did you do then?" the sheriff asked.

"I made sure that Mr. Alcott was still breathing and would be all right for a few minutes, then I ran for help. I met Miss Alcott on her way here. She went ahead to see to her father. I was winded, so I sent Mrs. Emerson's servant to fetch you. You know the rest."

The sheriff frowned. "You let Miss Alcott come here alone?"

With a rueful grin, Fred said, "Try to stop Louisa from doing what she wants."

"He couldn't have stopped me!" Louisa said in the same instant.

A smile flitted across Sheriff Staples's face. "Very well. Miss Alcott, what did you see when you got here?"

"My father was on the ground, holding his head." She glanced at her father, dozing on the bench. "Dr. Bartlett, are you sure he is all right? I'd like to bring him home."

Dr. Bartlett said, "He'll be fine for a few minutes."

The sheriff cleared his throat. "You didn't see anyone else, Miss Alcott? Or notice anything unusual?"

She shook her head.

"Did you hear the shot?"

"I was with Mrs. Emerson. We both heard it."

"Do you know what time it was?"

"I was thinking about that," she said. "I think it must have been nearly three o'clock."

"Thank you," he said, writing it down in a little notebook. "I'm sure Mrs. Emerson will confirm that."

The sheriff called his deputy over to Finch's body. They conferred in low voices. Louisa edged closer so she could overhear. She waited to see how competent this man was before she would reveal any of her own deductions.

"His pockets are turned out. This is most likely a robbery that went wrong," the sheriff said.

His deputy disagreed. "Who would come out here looking to rob someone? I think Alcott's story is suspicious. He might have a reason for shooting this fellow that we don't know about."

"Then where's the gun?" the sheriff asked.

"He had time to hide it," the deputy replied.

"But who hit him on the head?"

"Maybe he did it to himself," the deputy answered. "Alcott's one of those odd types. Maybe he got it into his head that he had to shoot somebody—we don't know how he thinks."

"John, we don't have nearly enough cause to charge a friend of Mr. Emerson's."

"Emerson is a fine gentleman. But he has funny taste in friends. Alcott's not even a Christian—the family doesn't go to church. I say we take him in and ask him some more questions."

Fred sidled over to Louisa and asked out the side of his mouth, "What's happening?"

"The sheriff thinks it's a robbery but the deputy wants to take Father to jail," she whispered back.

"What can we do?" Fred asked, his eyes darting nervously from Louisa to the sheriff and back again.

"Nothing," Louisa answered.

Fred began to protest, but Louisa hushed him with a quick warning look. The sheriff had turned his attention back to them.

"Miss Alcott," Sheriff Staples said, "I think you should go home. You must be distraught." His sharp eyes were watching her face closely as if to see if she was indeed upset.

"What about my father?" Louisa asked.

"I'd like to keep Mr. Alcott for questioning."

"Father is injured," Louisa cried. "Dr. Bartlett, you can't allow this!"

"Mr. Alcott should be at home in bed," Fred interjected.

"Louisa, don't worry," Dr. Bartlett said, patting her arm. "Our local jail has the reputation for being quite a pleasant place and Mr. Staples is a considerate jailer. I live right next door. With a blow to the head you want to keep a close eye on the patient."

"Then I'll go with him," Louisa said.

Dr. Bartlett shook his head. "If you don't mind me saying so, Miss Alcott, you look exhausted. Your father will get better care with me."

The sheriff said, "Your father will be home soon enough. Go home, Miss Alcott." His tone made it clear she had no choice.

Louisa knew she wouldn't prevail against both men. "Very well," she said. "But Sheriff Staples, have you considered how the rain confirms my father's story? His back is wet because he was lying facedown, unconscious, when it rained. After the gunshot."

The sheriff narrowed his eyes at her, then casually reached over to touch Bronson's back. "That's an interesting theory young lady. But even if I agree that he was unconscious during the rain . . . we don't know what he was doing when that gun went off."

"But it supports his story?" Louisa pressed.

"Possibly," the sheriff admitted.

Satisfied that she had made her point, Louisa turned to Fred. "Let's go home, Fred."

The sheriff held up a finger. "Not so fast. Mr. Llewellyn is an important witness. He was the first to find the body. We'll need him to write down what he saw."

Louisa stared at them all, furious. It was only because she was a girl that they wouldn't let her go to the jailhouse. "Very well, I'll go home alone."

"Wait," Fred said hurriedly. "Are we sure it's safe? The killer might be out there!"

The deputy and sheriff exchanged glances. "Perhaps I should escort her," the deputy said.

"For heaven's sake," Louisa exclaimed. "Either it's a robber who's long gone, or the killer is my father, which I don't believe for a minute, and you have him in custody! I'll be fine." She

stormed off, not southward, but by the northward path leading to Hillside.

"Louisa!" Fred called. "Be careful."

"Take care of my father," she called over her shoulder, taking
her eyes off the path. Her foot stepped on something and her
ankle twisted but she managed to stay upright.

She glanced down to see what obstacle had tripped her up.
It was a carved wooden horse, crude but familiar.

Casually she knelt down and acted as if she needed to lace
up her boot. Conscious of the eyes of the others on her, she
surreptitiously slipped the carving into the deep pocket of her
skirt. Then she straightened up and waved goodbye to Fred.

As soon as she was out of sight, she pulled out the horse. It
was Henry's work, she was sure of it. Her breath came in shal-
low and fast. Lidian had worried that Henry might turn
violent, but Louisa had dismissed her fears. Had she been
terribly wrong?

Her imagination took over, and in her mind's eye she could
see the scene so clearly. Henry had come to visit and talk with
Bronson. Often he came just to argue about the architectural
merits (or lack thereof) of the gazebo. Perhaps Finch had come
upon them and he had repeated his threats against Lidian.
Henry, pushed too far, had fought with him. In the melee,
somehow Finch's gun had gone off.

Faced with the dead man, Henry had quickly concocted a
plan with Bronson. He would strike Bronson over the head and
then Henry would run away. Bronson would plead ignorance

and no one would be able to prove anything. Except for the act of violence that started the whole chain in motion, it was the kind of harebrained scheme that philosophers might come up with when left to their own devices.

She knew she should give the carved horse to the sheriff; it was evidence. But she couldn't be the instrument of Henry's destruction. Nonsense, Louisa, she told herself. If Henry had done this, then he must also have hit her father over the head and stolen Finch's money and then run away like a coward. If he had done all these things, then he wasn't worthy of her protection. But need he be arrested on her evidence? Deciding to postpone the moment of decision, she slipped the horse back into her pocket and started for home.

Louisa wouldn't have noticed the basket to one side of the path, except that the white dishcloth stood out against the dark green undergrowth. She brushed aside the ferns and bushes and retrieved it. It was Beth's basket, the one she used to bring Father his lunch when he was working in the fields or at the gazebo.

She glanced inside the basket and saw it was empty except for the cloth and a few stray strawberries. Did that mean Beth had been at the gazebo, too? Why didn't Father say so? And why was it here, discarded in the woods? She grabbed the basket and began walking, faster and faster. Soon she was running. By the time Hillside was in view, she had a stitch in her side.

The sun had reemerged after the brief rain shower and she felt the perspiration drying tight and salty on her skin.

Through the window of the parlor, she could see Beth sewing her handkerchiefs. So Beth was home and safe. Father was in jail but getting the medical attention he needed. What about George?

She went to the barn and knocked on the secret door. There was no answer. She opened the door and found that George's room was empty. Her copy of *Robinson Crusoe* lay in the center of the bed.

So he had run. Flight made George look guilty; but on the other hand, what other chance of justice did he have? The laws of the United States had failed him. To gain his freedom, he had to run away.

If he had killed Finch, Louisa wondered whether she would be able to defend George. After all, Finch was an evil man and if anyone had the right to protect himself against Finch, surely it was George.

She wondered if her father and Fred would agree with her. She was certain the sheriff would not.

Louisa pressed her palms to the small of her back and stretched. She was so tired. No matter how much she told herself that George killing Finch was acceptable, she didn't believe it. She had been brought up to revere all life, even the life of an evil man like Finch.

Her mind returned to the clearing, recalling every detail. Suddenly, her chest felt hollow and her body began to shake. Moments before she saw Finch, his heart was pumping and he was breathing. Then he wasn't. The blood seeped through his clothing but it didn't flow in his veins. His blue eyes stared up at the sky, but they would never see again. Secure in the hidden room, Louisa let herself give in to the horror of what she had seen.

After her sobs had subsided, she rubbed her eyes with a corner of her skirt, tucked her loose hair behind her ears, and stood up. "That was pathetic and useless," she muttered. "I'm glad no one was here to see it."

Locking the barn behind her, she quietly let herself into the back door in the kitchen. The room was empty and she was grateful for another few moments before she had to face Beth and tell her everything that had happened.

As she replaced Beth's basket on its hook, a large ceramic bowl full of new strawberries on the table caught her eye. She pumped cold water into a tin cup and splashed her face. Her eyes closed, Louisa groped for the kitchen towel. Someone placed it in her hand.

Louisa smiled. She dried her face and opened her eyes to see dear sweet Beth standing in front of her.

"Where have you been?" Beth asked. "I have something awful to tell you!"

CHAPTER SEVENTEEN

*Jo had the least self-control, and had hard
times trying to curb the fiery spirit which was
continually getting her into trouble . . . Her sisters
used to say that they rather liked to get Jo into a
fury because she was such an angel afterward.*

ot as awful as my news," Louisa said flatly.

"Louy, you always have to be more tragic and melodramatic than everyone else in the family!" Beth said, uncharacteristically peevish. "I've been waiting for hours to tell you what happened."

Louisa took pity on her sister and sat down and patted the chair next to her. Besides, maybe Beth's story would give Louisa some clues.

"I picked strawberries today," Beth began.

"I noticed."

"Here, have some." Momentarily distracted, Beth pushed the bowl full of berries in front of Louisa. She waited until Louisa popped one in her mouth. They were small and sweet and Louisa, anxious as she was, couldn't help but savor them on her tongue.

Satisfied, Beth went on. "I brought a sandwich and some berries up to the gazebo for Father's dinner just before one o'clock."

Louisa thought back. So when she and Fred had returned to Hillside, Beth must have just left. "That was very thoughtful," Louisa said.

"Father didn't think so," Beth said. "As soon as I arrived he tried to get me to leave. But Miss Whittaker's card said she would come in at one o'clock. So I tried to stay. Finally Father grew angry and yelled at me to go home." Her chin trembled. "He never gets angry with me."

"No one does, Beth, dear," Louisa said, stroking her sister's hand. "What did you do then?" Louisa chose another strawberry and bit down, enjoying the burst of flavor. It had been too long since she had eaten those scones.

"I had no choice but to go. But I ran into Miss Whittaker on the path. She's met me several times, but she acted as though she didn't know me." Beth jumped up and began to pace up about the kitchen. "How dare she?"

"She's quite awful," Louisa agreed.

"I wanted to keep an eye on her and Father, but I couldn't once he told me to go home." Beth gave Louisa an accusing glance. "You were supposed to keep them from being alone together."

Louisa ran through the events of the day in her mind. After all that had happened, Beth scolding her was the final straw. "Beth, I was busy."

"Too busy walking and visiting with Fred," Beth cried. "You always please yourself instead of doing what's right."

Louisa felt an inevitable anger rise up in her. Staring down at the strawberry hulls on the table, she cried, "Finch, the slave catcher, has been murdered. Fred discovered the body. Father says he didn't do it because someone hit him over the head and knocked him unconscious, but Sheriff Staples doesn't believe his story and put him in jail. If Father didn't kill him, then to my mind the two lead suspects are George or Henry. That's how I've been pleasing myself this afternoon. Are you happy now?"

As soon as she finished her litany, she looked up to see the effect of her words. Beth was ashen and had to steady herself with a hand on the table.

A wave of shame engulfed Louisa. "Oh, Beth, I'm so sorry," she said. "I never should have told you like that. Father is fine. He just has a little bump on his head. And the only reason he's at the jailhouse is because Dr. Bartlett thought he could care for Father better there."

"The slave catcher is dead?" Beth asked weakly.

Louisa nodded.

"How?"

"He was shot, probably with his own gun," Louisa said. She related everything that had happened that day, omitting only her private conversations with Fred. As a final flourish, she pulled Henry's wooden horse out of her pocket and plunked it down on the table.

"Why would Father tell you no one had visited him?" Beth wondered, focusing on her small part in the drama.

"Probably he didn't want to admit that Miss Whittaker was there, too," Louisa said without considering the effect of her words on Beth.

"Louisa, you should be ashamed of yourself," Beth cried. "You always believe the worst about Father. You can't just love him and be proud of him the way I am, and Marmee, too. You always have to *judge*."

To Louisa, Beth's words cut like a sharp knife slicing through cheese. The habit of protecting Beth extended to more than her health; Louisa felt responsible for Beth's innocent nature, too. "Beth, you're too young to understand."

"No, I'm not. I know why you are angry with Father. And its not about Miss Whittaker. I remember Fruitlands, too."

Fruitlands. Louisa cast her mind back, remembering her father's grand experiment in communal living. Within six months the provisions and the money had run out. Louisa's memories of that winter were so powerful that her fingers felt the chill of the unheated attic and her stomach ached from too little food. The experiment had nearly torn the family apart.

"Beth, I'm angry for all of us. Father let us pay the price for his ideals."

"At least he *has* ideals," Beth said. "I admire that and I thought you did, too."

"I did—I *do*," Louisa said. "But the family should matter, too. And if he's made a fool of himself with Miss Whittaker— after all Marmee has done for him—then I can't forgive him for that."

"I don't think he would ever betray Marmee," Beth said. "He adores her."

Louisa recalled how sweetly Marmee and her father had said farewell. "Perhaps you're right," she admitted.

Beth glared a moment longer, then relented and gave her sister a quick hug. Louisa immediately felt better; she couldn't bear to be at odds with Beth.

"That's better. Beth, tell me what you think we should do. Can we trust the sheriff? If George killed the man sent to catch him, it would be self-defense, wouldn't it? After all, Finch was an evil man. And George has suffered so much."

"George wouldn't do such a thing!"

"Then where is he?" Louisa shot back. "And if it isn't George, then it might be Henry. Why should I find justice for a slave catcher if one of our friends has to pay the price?"

Beth's face was full of dismay. "Louy, think of what you are saying. If Finch was killed by a stranger, or by Miss Whittaker, would you want them to be punished?"

"Of course," Louisa muttered, her eyes fixed on the faded pattern on the rug.

"So the only difference between Miss Whittaker being guilty and Henry being innocent is that we like Henry more?"

"Perhaps." Louisa drummed her heels against the sofa. There was no doubt in her mind that Beth was the very best of them. She was the true North of Louisa's moral compass. "No wonder Father calls you the Conscience," she said with a sigh. "Very well, Beth. The whole truth and only the truth is our goal."

Beth's pale white hand found Louisa's tanned one. "You aren't alone. I'll be here with you. What will you do first?"

Louisa pressed her palms into her eyes. "I don't know," she wailed. "I'm so tired."

Beth straightened up and jabbed her elbow into Louisa's side until she sat up straight, too. "You can do it, Louy. Why don't you make a list of people who have reason to want Finch dead?"

"But I barely knew him!" Louisa protested. "What if some stranger killed him?"

"Then a stranger killed him." Beth spoke simply, tilting her head to one side. "We can only try to solve the problems within our reach. We'll make a list of Mr. Finch's enemies. If we clear them all, then the murderer has to be a stranger."

"Mr. X!" Louisa interjected. The sobriquet appealed to the sensationalist in her.

Beth couldn't help smiling. "Then Mr. X will make himself known. Get some paper."

Louisa took the wooden horse and headed for the parlor, Beth at her heels. She found a sheet of paper, a pen, and a bottle of ink and installed herself at the small writing table next to the sofa. "Number one," she said. "I suppose that has to be George."

Beth's hand went to the hollow of her throat. "I hope it's not George."

"Who has a better reason to want Finch gone? He was at the gazebo and he's run away." Louisa went to the window and looked at the barn, looming against the darkening sky. She wanted to go out and look for George, but if he had killed Finch, then he was probably long gone.

Beth's face reflected the worry Louisa felt. "Who's next?"

"Well, I think Finch was blackmailing Mr. Pryor about his illegal liquor," Louisa said. "And Mr. Pryor was missing from the tavern today, just about the time that Father was at the gazebo."

"That's good. Put him down for number two."

"And Miss Whittaker, of course. She and Finch have some sort of sordid history. They argued last night at the hotel. And she was not herself when I saw her today. I believe she had strawberry stains on her skirt—perhaps she struggled with Finch."

"She was at the gazebo only an hour or so before you say the shot was fired. Even if Father lied about her visit." Beth wrapped a blanket about her shoulders tightly enough to ward off any bad news.

"Don't forget she's leaving the hotel. Let's call her number three. Now there's Henry and Lidian. They both have excellent reasons for wanting Finch gone. But Lidian was with me when the shot was fired."

"That's a relief," Beth said.

"But I don't know where Henry was."

"But the only reason you think Henry was there is that wooden horse," Beth pointed out. "Are you sure it's the same one Henry carved this morning?"

Louisa ran her hands over the rough carving. "It looks the same, but Henry is always carving animals." She felt some of the load on her heart lighten. "For all we know, Henry dropped this one weeks ago at the gazebo."

"But still, he's number four."

Louisa marked down his name, but she deliberately made it fainter than the others. "Now what about Father?"

"Why would Father kill Finch?" Beth protested. "He had never even met him."

"But Father is hiding something. I say he's on the list."

Beth frowned. "Then in that case you had better put your name down, too. Finch was threatening everyone you held dear."

"Fine." Louisa jabbed her pen nib into the paper, making a blot that spread across the other names. "I hope you don't expect me to investigate myself?"

"Of course not," Beth said with a teasing smile.

"What about you?" Louisa said. "My motive is your motive, too. And you were there."

Beth's smile faded. "That's not funny, Louy."

"All right, then, what about Fred?"

"Fred?" Louisa shook off the suggestion. "When Fred arrived at the gazebo, Finch was already dead. And Fred would never ever hurt Father."

Beth nodded with a relieved smile.

Louisa ran her finger down the list. "This is a long list."

"Gracious," Beth exclaimed. "Mr. Finch was only in town for a few days."

"He was a nasty man."

CHAPTER EIGHTEEN

"I don't think secrets agree with me, I feel
rumpled up in my mind
since you told me that," said Jo rather ungratefully.

*L*ouisa propped her feet up on the sofa. She plumped a pillow under her head and let her eyelids sink shut. It was a delicious relief to rest after all that had happened that day.

"Louy!" Beth said, poking her sister with a pointed finger. Louisa sat up, startled.

"You can't sleep now," Beth said. "You have to solve this mystery before someone innocent suffers."

"Beth, leave me be," Louisa answered, not opening her eyes. "I'm exhausted. Father is safe. Fred is with him at the jail but he'll be home soon. I can't do anything about George because I don't know where he is. The mystery can wait until tomorrow."

Beth didn't answer. The silence grew and grew until it weighed too heavy on Louisa's eyelids. Slowly, she opened one eye. Beth was staring at her expectantly.

"Just a little nap? Please?" Louisa begged. "It's almost six o'clock—there's nothing I can do at this hour."

"You need to question Miss Whittaker before she leaves town. And you must do it before Father comes home."

Beth was right; Father would demand that his daughters nurse him once he was home. Spending time in jail would only aggravate his sense of injury.

Louisa opened the other eye. "You won't let me rest until I go, will you?"

*   *   *

On her way into town, Louisa walked at less than her usual brisk pace. She had often bragged of walking twenty miles in a day, but today she was bone tired. She deliberately passed the Emersons' house on the far side of the street.

"Louisa! Louisa! Wait!"

Louisa gritted her teeth at the unwelcome sound of Lidian's voice. Reluctantly, she turned back.

Lidian, dressed in a housedress and a pair of elegant slippers, hurried out from the side entrance to the house. She rushed through the front garden and waited at the gate. Once Louisa was close enough, Lidian grabbed her wrist and whispered, "Is it true?" Her eyes were fixed on Louisa's face, eager for news.

"Is what true?" Louisa snapped.

Lidian made an exasperated noise. "That awful man Finch is dead. Is it true? Please let it be true!"

"It is true." Louisa bit back all the words she wanted to say. Like "Shame on you," or "What would Waldo Emerson think of such a sentiment?" But she controlled her tongue. "How did you hear?"

"Everyone in town knows." Lidian looked surprised. "But no one is saying who killed him. Do you know?"

"I don't," Louisa said. "But do you know where I can find Henry? I have to talk to him."

"About Finch?" Lidian's beautiful brown eyes narrowed suspiciously. "But you said Henry would never hurt anyone."

"I still have to talk with him. It's important."

"About the murder?"

"No," Louisa lied.

Lidian gnawed on her knuckle. "I haven't spoken to him since I saw you at Walden Pond."

Louisa turned to go. "If you see him, tell him to find me as soon as possible."

Louisa sped off, leaving Lidian on the street in her slippers. Ten minutes later she stood outside the Middlesex Hotel looking at the entrance. What was the best way to get the answers she needed? Miss Whittaker was an accomplished liar.

She was still standing there, unclear as to her best next step, when there was a tap on her shoulder. Startled, she whirled around. It was Mr. Pryor. She took a step back. It was one thing, she decided, to speculate in theory about how someone might be a murderer. It was a much different thing to run into one of your suspects in the street.

In a low voice, Pryor said, "Have you heard the news? The man who was so interested in our package has been killed."

"I know," she said.

"It's terrible, of course," he said. "But I must own it's a relief." He paused. "Don't you agree?"

Shame on all of us, Louisa thought. Out loud she said, "Certainly. It will make things much simpler."

Mr. Pryor nodded. "And just in time, too—the other packages are due to arrive in two days."

"So soon?" Louisa asked. How quickly things had changed. Yesterday this would have been good news. But today George was missing and Louisa suspected him of murder. If the sheriff knew of George's existence he wouldn't look any further for the murderer.

"What is the matter, Miss Alcott?" He looked closely at her face. "I thought you would be pleased. Without Finch around, we should have no problem getting our shipment safely North."

"Yes, about that. I came to talk to you today about the package at one o'clock. But you weren't there. Which seemed odd since it is such a busy time for your tavern." She paused. "I was worried about you, since you and Finch argued today, not long before he was killed."

Pryor started to object, but Louisa touched his hand and said in her most sympathetic manner, "Mr. Pryor, your argument was overheard."

He swallowed hard. "You think I might be suspected of killing him?"

Louisa shrugged. "Do you have an alibi?"

Pryor gave her a sharp look.

"Tell me where you were this afternoon."

Prior's worried face lightened. "Come, I'll show you."

Louisa hesitated before following him down the alley. But there were people in the street and in the tavern. Together they marched down the alley to the back entrance of the tavern. Surely she was safe. Inside, there were a few men drinking at the bar. They stared at Louisa but she kept her chin high and followed Pryor into his small office. He pulled a long envelope from his desk and handed it to her. It was full of banknotes.

"Finch was threatening to report me to Sam Staples for not paying my liquor taxes. He demanded a high price for his silence. So this afternoon I went to my bank in Lexington to get the money. I was supposed to give it to him tonight."

"And someone can verify this?"

"I took the coach into Lexington. I knew at least two people on the ride." And then there's the money." He gestured to the stack of notes. "Of course, I don't want this to get out, but I will confess to it if need be."

Louisa's mind worked frantically. It was no great surprise that Finch was a blackmailer. She was inclined to think Pryor's story was true—otherwise, why tell Louisa about the taxes? And if it was, then Pryor didn't kill Finch. Ironically, his alibi for murder was that he was arranging to pay his blackmailer, who just happened to be the victim. "Very well," she said. Mentally, she scratched his name off the list of suspects. "I accept your explanation."

Prior nodded sharply. "Good. Now, I hope this won't distract us from our true business. Just after sunset on the day after tomorrow, I'll come to your barn with the other packages. We'll get them settled for the night and then we'll send them North."

It was on the tip of Louisa's tongue to confess that George was missing, but she held back. Maybe George would return. If not, she didn't relish having to tell George's wife and children that he was a murderer. Time enough to tell Pryor everything the next day.

Leaving the tavern by the same discreet door, she returned to her survey of the Middlesex Hotel. There was nothing to do but go straight up to Miss Whittaker's room and confront her. If she didn't know about the murder, then the news ought to shock her into speaking freely. If she did know, it might be for the simplest of reasons: Miss Whittaker was the killer.

She entered the hotel and spied Judith wiping down a table in the crowded restaurant. She went to the door and beckoned to her.

"Miss Alcott! Back again?" Judith said, surprised and with a pitying look at Louisa's dress.

"Not for the restaurant," Louisa assured her. "I couldn't possibly clean up twice in one day. What I need to know is which room Miss Whittaker is in. I'd rather not ask at the desk."

Judith looked puzzled but she answered freely. "That's easy, Miss. Room 201. It's the best room." She lowered her voice, "Miss Louisa, did you hear the news? That man who was arguing with Miss Whittaker—they found him dead!"

Did everyone know? "Yes, I heard," Louisa said. "Shocking," she added perfunctorily. "I must go. Thank you, Judith."

Louisa hurried up the stairs before the officious-looking man at the front desk could ask her business. Dashing down the long carpeted hall, she found Room 201. She steeled herself for what was bound to be a trying encounter and knocked.

There was no answer. She knocked again. Miss Whittaker must be out. Glancing up and down the hall to be sure she wasn't observed, she tried the door handle. But it was locked.

She slumped onto a bench in the hall, trying to decide what to do next. A voice singing around the corner caught her attention. A moment later a maid in a dark uniform came round the corner carrying a pile of towels. She was young, with a pretty round face and a taste for jolly songs.

Louisa tried to recall her conversation with Judith at lunch. What was her friend's name? "Sally?" she asked, hesitant as if she was ready to be mistaken.

The maid stopped singing, her face scarlet. "Miss, I'm sorry. I know I shouldn't sing."

Louisa waved that concern away. "Why shouldn't you sing while you work? Everyone should. Is your name Sally?"

"Yes, Miss." Sally was clearly confused. "Have I done something wrong?"

"No, no. Judith was telling me about you today at lunch. My name is Louisa Alcott."

"Miss Alcott! Your ma saved Judith's father's life. She talks about your family all the time."

"Sit down," Louisa said, patting the bench next to her.

"Oh, I couldn't do that," Sally said.

"Then I'll stand, too," Louisa said, getting to her feet. "I need to get into Miss Whittaker's room. It's important."

"Is that all?" Sally asked. "After what you did for Judith, I'd be glad to help you. I have the master key to all the rooms."

"I don't want to get you in trouble," Louisa began.

"That Miss Whittaker is up to no good—all the girls agree. She's sweet as pie to men, but we women know better. Besides, the manager wants her out of the hotel. He won't believe anything she says." Checking that no one was watching, Sally pulled out her master key and with a deft turn, the door was open.

"There you go, Miss," she said. "And please . . ."

"If I'm caught, I don't know you!" Louisa said. "Thank you." Sally disappeared down the hall, humming cheerfully.

Louisa slipped into the spacious room. Miss Whittaker had not skimped on her accommodations. Besides a large bed, there was a sitting area and a desk next to the window. Everywhere were signs of hurried packing. The dress Miss Whittaker had been wearing earlier was tossed across the back of a chair. Louisa examined the skirt, confirming her suspicions about the strawberries.

She went to the desk and looked through the papers there. She found letters from gentlemen in New York. They seemed to be her backers for the magazine project. One of her correspondents mentioned how pleased he was that Emerson, Thoreau, and Alcott were writing essays for the magazine, and he agreed to reimburse her for the printing expenses of $1,450. Louisa frowned. As far as she knew there had been no printing. In fact, not a single essay had yet been written.

She shuffled through the rest of the papers and found a pile of blank invoices from a printing shop. One was partially filled out for the amount of $450.

Louisa sank down in the plush armchair in front of the desk. Miss Whittaker was swindling her investors with falsified bills. And she was hiding behind the reputations of Louisa's friends and father to do it.

Mr. Emerson could probably weather such a scandal once it was made public, but what about Bronson Alcott? It would ruin his already shaky reputation.

"That little witch," Louisa muttered.

She must have done something similar in Washington and Finch had known about it. Louisa knew Finch wouldn't hesitate to blackmail Miss Whittaker. Which gave Miss Whittaker ample motive to get rid of Finch. But what about the gun?

Louisa began checking under the furniture and felt all the crannies of the upholstery. She returned to the desk and began rummaging through the papers. So intent was she on her search, she didn't hear the door open.

CHAPTER NINETEEN

*I've got sense, if I haven't style, which is more than
some people have.*

"Miss Alcott, can I help you find what you are looking for?"

Louisa's back stiffened straight. Her right hand reached for
the compromising invoice. She slipped it into her pocket and
turned around. Miss Whittaker, once again impeccably dressed
and coiffed, filled the doorway, Louisa's only exit from the room.

"What are you doing here?" Miss Whittaker's angry,
clipped words were at odds with her ladylike demeanor.

With a tilt of her chin, Louisa said simply, "I'm searching your room."

"Your honesty is refreshing." Miss Whittaker's eyes glinted with appreciation. "How did you get in?" She removed her key from the door and carefully placed it in her large purse. Louisa eyed it warily; did the purse also contain a gun?

"The door was open," Louisa lied. "You weren't here, so I let myself in."

"And then you were struck by the urge to snoop through my papers?"

Louisa moved away from the desk toward the window. Miss Whittaker didn't take her eyes off her. "Miss Whittaker, can you explain these false invoices for services never rendered? It looks very suspicious."

Miss Whittaker put down her purse and sat down on the settee in the middle of the room. "I created a fairy tale for some gullible investors. They're great admirers of these Transcendentalist philosophers, and they loved the idea of having their own magazine. I may have also suggested that Mr. Emerson might speak at their clubs and dine at their homes. They were more than happy to write checks for a magazine I had no intention of publishing."

Louisa's mouth had fallen open. "You admit it?"

Miss Whittaker shrugged her elegant shoulders. "It's over now. I'm done."

Louisa sat opposite her on a plush armchair. "Would your decision have anything to do with Mr. Finch?"

Miss Whittaker eyed her with speculation. "For a frowsy country miss, you seem to know everything."

"What I lack in style I make up for with inquisitiveness," Louisa said. "Finch knew you were a swindler?"

Miss Whittaker snorted. "Knew? We had worked together before, hoodwinking some stamp collectors in Washington out of thousands."

"Did he threaten to expose you?" Louisa kept her voice light and conversational, but her stomach was churning. Miss Whittaker was confessing to the perfect motive. Was Louisa chatting with a murderer?

"You would think he'd let me alone for old times' sake," Miss Whittaker said bitterly. "But he wanted a percentage for doing nothing but keeping quiet. I wouldn't give it to him. I've worked too hard. Do you have any idea how boring it is trying to charm philosophers? They only want to be told how intelligent they are."

Louisa blinked. "The only men I know are philosophers," she admitted. "Why are you telling me all this?"

"Why not? The law can't touch me for something I only planned to do." Miss Whittaker frowned. "I never collected any money from anyone. Unfortunately. And now that Finch is dead, I've nothing to fear."

"How did you know he was dead?" Louisa asked.

"It's all anyone can talk about downstairs." Miss Whittaker took a pin out of her hairdressing and all of her hair fell about her shoulders. She massaged her scalp with her fingertips. "That's better. Maybe it's worth looking as unkempt as you for the sake of being comfortable."

Ignoring the jibe, Louisa studied Miss. Whittaker. "You had an appointment with my father today," she stated.

"Did I?" Miss Whittaker yawned delicately.

"Yes, you did." Louisa said. She stood up and went to Miss Whittaker's discarded skirt. She held it up. "Look. For all someone has tried to clean them, these are strawberry stains. And they are the first of the crop, just like the ones my sister picked this morning. No hotel restaurant has these. You were in the clearing where Finch was murdered."

Miss Whittaker didn't look nervous; rather, she stretched her arms and legs out like a cat and said, "When did he die?"

"Not long after your appointment with my father," Louisa said.

Miss Whittaker raised a single eyebrow. "I was in the hotel by half past one. You know I was. You saw me when I returned."

"You might have left and gone back," Louisa said.

Miss Whittaker shook her head with an irritating grin. "That terrible maid who's always making such a noise with her singing came in and I had her try to clean the skirt. She was in and out of here for the next hour. Then I went downstairs with a book to the lounge. At least five people saw me there."

Louisa rubbed her temples, trying to work out the times. "If you knew you couldn't be connected to Finch's murder, why did you lie about seeing Father?"

"I have a soft spot for the foolish man." She shot Louisa a conspiratorial look. "Bronson is terribly good-looking. And Finch was very trying. If Bronson shot him, he did me a favor. "

"What do you mean?" Louisa turned to stare. "Why would Father kill Finch? He hadn't even met the man!"

Miss Whittaker's eyes opened wide, like an innocent child. "While we were nibbling on strawberries, I told him everything. He wasn't pleased with me, but I soon convinced him to forgive me. Then I told Bronson that Finch is a wanted man in Maryland. A delicious irony, don't you think, that a wanted man was chasing a fugitive? Bronson and I had a lovely earnest talk about it. But Bronson would certainly have informed the authorities. And from my experience with the man, I can tell you Finch would have taken exception to being arrested."

"But how would Finch know that my father knew anything damaging about him?" Louisa asked.

Miss Whittaker's eyes widened even further and her lips curved into a reminiscent smile. "I told him, of course. On my way back to the hotel, I ran into him on the street. The problem with Concord is that there are so few streets. Anyway, I took great pleasure in telling him that not only would he not get a penny from me, but that your father would happily put him in jail."

Louisa felt a chill run down her spine. In a quiet voice that her sisters knew well and feared, she asked, "And did you know that Finch had a gun?"

Miss Whittaker shrugged.

"You are despicable," Louisa spat. Without waiting for an answer, she said, "It wasn't enough to embroil the finest men in the country in your fraud: You sent a dangerous criminal after my father."

Miss Whittaker rose to her feet in a languid movement, as though it was almost too much effort. She went to the door, clearly expecting Louisa to leave. "This conversation is beginning to bore me. Your father is fine."

"He's in jail!" Louisa said, wanting to somehow pierce the woman's self-possession.

"Really?" Miss Whittaker said, her lovely eyes widening. "Well, he won't be there for long, will he? Unless he killed Finch . . . But even then, the town will probably give him a medal. Finch was a nasty man."

"And so are his associates," Louisa said, not bothering to disguise her disdain. She went through the door, and as though struck by an afterthought, she said, "I hope you're leaving town immediately."

"It depends. With Finch gone, I might stay. Bronson still admires me; he won't want to tarnish my reputation."

"You can count equally on me to do the opposite," Louisa warned. "You forgot about the falsified invoice. I have it."

Miss Whittaker went perfectly still, her eyes darting to the desk.

Louisa went on. "If you aren't out of town on the first train tomorrow, I'll bring it to Mr. Emerson. He won't hesitate to bring it to the authorities. Unlike my foolish father, Mr. Emerson isn't susceptible to your charms."

Miss Whittaker sighed elegantly. "Well, I suppose I don't have a choice. Never mind; I have another project in Philadelphia." As she waited to close the door behind Louisa, she said, "I don't often underestimate people, particularly women. Perhaps we'll meet again, Miss Alcott."

The door shut with a bang. Louisa leaned against it and muttered, "Not if I have any choice in the matter."

Louisa made her way downstairs and through the lobby, thinking furiously. Thanks to Miss Whittaker's candor, Louisa knew a lot more about what had happened and why. The more she learned, the more depressed she got. Unless Miss Whittaker had convinced several people to lie, she couldn't have killed Finch. Louisa crossed her off the rapidly shrinking list.

She stepped into the street. Across the way the Wright Tavern was overflowing with men drinking away the hard work of the day. Behind her the hotel restaurant was full, too.

All the shops and offices were shuttered for the night and the street was mostly quiet.

"Louisa!"

A voice behind her made her jump before she recognized Fred's voice. "Fred, don't frighten me like that," she said tiredly. "I've had an excruciatingly long day."

"Me, too," he said sourly, reminding her that he had been at the jailhouse giving a statement.

"I'm sorry!" she exclaimed. "While I've been investigating, you've had a much more tedious time. How is Father?"

"The doctor thinks he's fine and made him go to bed. Bronson didn't even argue; he just wanted to sleep. The doctor is keeping an eye on him tonight."

"I'm so glad to see you," she said. Tucking her arm in his and turning toward home, she asked, "How did you find me?"

"I went back to Hillside. Beth told me where to find you." With an exasperated sigh, he said, "You do realize how foolish it was to see Miss Whittaker alone, don't you?"

"Why wouldn't I?" Louisa asked, but recalling her fears about a gun, she didn't dare meet his eyes.

"She might be a killer, that's why!"

"She's not," Louisa interrupted. "She was here at the hotel when Finch was shot. My list of suspects is getting shorter."

"Damnation," Fred said. "I thought she was a good prospect. This makes things look even worse."

"For Father?" Louisa's stomach had a cold, hard knot whenever she thought about her father's role in the day's events.

"Bronson Alcott a murderer?" Fred exclaimed. "Louisa, you and your father have your differences, but you can't believe that of him. Besides, he was unconscious."

"How can we be sure?" Louisa asked, tightening her grip on his arm.

"Because I saw him lying on the ground. Someone hit him on the head and then killed Finch. I'm sure of it." His voice dropped. "And we both know who."

"Not Henry!" Louisa almost wailed. "He wouldn't do such a thing, even if he was there."

"Henry?" Fred looked baffled. "What are you talking about? Henry couldn't possibly have shot Finch."

"But he was there," Louisa said, miserable. "I found the horse he was carving in the clearing."

Fred's eyebrows knitted as he considered this new information. "But Henry's in jail!"

Louisa stopped dead in the road and tugged on Fred's elbow so he swung around and looked her in the face. "Jail? He's been arrested? How could you not tell me?"

Fred started to laugh. "Yes, Henry's in jail. But not for murder! He's been arrested for not paying his taxes!"

"He hasn't paid for years," Louisa said. "Until the war in Mexico is over, he says he won't let his tax dollars support it.

Nor the expansion of slavery into the Western territories. Are you saying that today, of all days, Sheriff Staples put him in jail?"

"Right after we left him this morning he had the bad luck to run into the sheriff. He's been locked up ever since, so Henry couldn't have been killing anyone."

They were approaching Hillside and Fred led her into the garden rather than the house. He sat on a bench and gestured to her to take her place next to him.

"We should go in to Beth; she must be frantic," Louisa said.

"I made sure she went to bed," Fred said. "She looked feverish. This has been too much for her. So we can talk out here for a moment. You have to face the unpleasant truth."

"Which one?" Louisa asked. She leaned against him, taking comfort in his sturdy shoulder.

She felt his body tense as he said in a hesitant voice, "There is only one man left who would kill Finch."

"No, he wouldn't . . ." Louisa's voice trailed off. What did she really know about George?

Fred ticked off his arguments on his fingers. "George's motive is stronger than anyone else's. He's a big man who could have struck down your father and wrestled the gun away from Finch."

"We don't even know he was there," Louisa protested, but she couldn't help remembering that load of twisted wood.

"We do." Fred's face was stern. "I was able to speak to Bronson alone. He told me that when he first recovered consciousness, he saw George running away from the clearing."

"Oh, no," Louisa moaned. "Did Father tell Sheriff Staples?"

"No. And he doesn't want us to, either. He said none of us could imagine the weight of slavery on a man's soul, and no one could be blamed for doing anything to avoid being recaptured."

"But Father can't condone murder; it violates all his principles."

"So does slavery," Fred pointed out. "I think he's choosing the lesser of two evils. Besides, we don't know what happened. It might have been self-defense."

"Then why did he hit Father first?" Louisa asked. "Only someone planning to kill Finch would do that."

"Maybe not . . ." Fred started slowly, but his words sped up as he developed his theory. "Finch had a good reason to want your father incapacitated, or worse, to buy some time to get out of town. So Finch hit your father and George might have seen it. George would have defended Bronson. In the struggle, Finch's gun went off." He took Louisa's hand. "It's understandable, but the law wouldn't make allowances. Right now Sheriff Staples is inclined to his theory that some stranger robbed and killed Finch. I say we let that story stand."

"Even if he took a man's life?" Louisa asked, incredulous.

"But wasn't Finch trying to do the same? Even worse than death was the fate waiting for George if he returned to his owner. I'd call it self-defense and get a good night's sleep." He stood up and held out his hand. She hesitated, her lower lip caught between her teeth.

"If George doesn't come back we'll know."

"He wouldn't abandon his children," she said slowly.

"But he could find them in Canada once all the fuss dies down," Fred pointed out. "Louisa, don't make things more difficult. If George killed Finch, he shouldn't have to suffer for it."

Louisa grabbed Fred's hand and let him pull her to her feet. "I wish there was someone who felt sorry that Finch was dead. I know that I should be outraged that his life was taken from him, but really all I feel is relief," she admitted.

Fred drew her close and encircled her with his arms. "Sometimes you have to choose between being a philosopher or a human being." His hold was loose and she knew he would let her go if she asked. Instead, she pressed her cheek against his chest.

His arms tightened and his lips touched her hair. "I want to ask you something important," he whispered.

"Not yet," Louisa said. "I can't think about the future with all this swirling about us. When it's over, we can talk."

"I'll hold you to that," he warned. They stood together for a few minutes as the moon rose, bathing them in its pale light.

"Louisa," Fred whispered.

"Yes?"

"This hair net you wear is perhaps the least romantic piece of clothing ever imagined."

She burst out laughing, grateful for his levity. Gently shoving him aside, she walked toward the house. "Come in," she said over her shoulder. "Tomorrow is soon enough to solve this mystery."

CHAPTER TWENTY

*For tunately it was early, and they went
through back streets,
so few people saw them, and no one laughed
at the queer party.*

*L*ouisa's thick sleep was interrupted by a familiar tapping on the wall outside. The woodpecker seemed intent on waking her. She sat up in her narrow bed, dislodging Goethe the kitten.

"I'm sorry," she whispered, scratching the cat's head. "I haven't been around much lately, have I?" Goethe's favorite spot was to curl up next to her while she wrote. She glanced at her writing desk and her abandoned novel. Until Finch's murder was solved, Louisa doubted she would be doing any writing. The cat, as well as her heroine, would have to wait.

She hopped out of bed and stretched, hands reaching toward the ceiling, working out all the kinks in her back from a long night's rest. She couldn't recall ever sleeping so deeply.

Peeking out the window, she saw that the sun was just coming up, casting the garden in a pale pink light. The woodpecker had moved on to the chicken coop, and she could hear the outraged clucking of the hens. Pulling her quilt off the bed, Louisa wrapped it around her shoulders, slipped her feet into her boots, and went outside to enjoy the dawn. She climbed the hill path to the bench where she and Fred had kissed. Could it have been only two nights ago?

Tucking the blanket around her, she waited for the sun to finish its arriving. She heard the woodpecker again, but it took her a few moments to find him. He'd moved to the woodshed and now was flitting toward the tree that housed their post office. Louisa hoped that the woodpecker wouldn't do any lasting harm to the tree trunk.

Tap, tap, tap. The woodpecker was industrious and even from where she sat, Louisa could see the small door to the post office pop open. Feeling the chill from her nose down to the stockingless toes, she stood up and started down. She stopped at the post office, intending to close it tightly, when she noticed something inside. Gingerly, she stuck her hand in and felt a hard object wrapped in a linen handkerchief. She unfolded the cloth to reveal a gun.

*   *   *

As Louisa hoped, Beth was the first downstairs.

"It's odd, isn't it, without Father or Marmee here?" Beth asked. Her face was pale and there were dark shadows around her eyes. "I don't like it one bit. When will Father return?"

"I'm leaving in a few minutes to fetch him. He's bound to look a mess, and I'd rather the streets were empty when I bring him back. The town already thinks we're mad." She gestured to the teapot on the table. "I've made tea."

Beth poured herself a cup, added some honey harvested from Bronson's hives, and drank it thirstily. "Did you see Miss Whittaker last night?" she asked.

Louisa nodded. "She's innocent. Of the murder, at least. Otherwise she is a perfectly dreadful woman who wanted to use Father and Mr. Emerson to cheat people." She explained everything that had happened, finishing with Fred's theory from the night before.

"Do you agree with Fred?" Beth asked in tears. "Did George kill that man?"

Louisa opened the drawer where she had hidden the gun. First she pulled out the handkerchief, knowing that the pistol would frighten Beth. "What do you think of this?" she asked.

"Why, that's one of my handkerchiefs," Beth said, her brow furrowed. She took it and examined it closer. "Yes, I embroidered this for George. What is this dirt?" She rubbed at a gray stain and held up a finger dirty with an oily mark. Louisa was silent.

"Louy, what does George's handkerchief have to do with anything?"

Louisa swallowed hard. "I found it in our post office. It was wrapped around a gun. That mark is gun oil."

Beth thrust the handkerchief away from her and rushed to the water pump and began scrubbing her hands with a rough cloth. When they were raw and splotched with red, she finally stopped and turned to her sister. "Did George do it?" she asked, in a voice that begged Louisa to lie to her.

Louisa put her arms around Beth and held her close. "I don't see any other explanation, Beth. He must have shot Finch, then used the handkerchief to clean his hands. He hid it before he ran away."

"But how did he know about the post office?" Beth asked. "That's our secret."

"Maybe he found it? Maybe Fred or Father told him about it." Louisa shrugged. "But to my mind that handkerchief is the final piece of the puzzle."

Beth started to shake, and Louisa realized she was quietly sobbing.

"I know, Beth, I don't like it, either. But George was pushed farther than anyone ought to be. Killing Finch was necessary to protect his own life. He has to think of his family." Beth's sobs subsided a little. "And at least we won't have to see him tried and sent to jail. He's long gone from here."

Beth stepped back. Rubbing her tears away with her fists, she looked like a small, frightened child. "I want Father," she said. "Louy, please bring Father home."

Louisa kissed Beth on the cheek. "I'll go now," she promised.

"Should you take Fred with you?" Beth asked.

"Let him sleep," Louisa decided. "I have to ask Father some hard questions, and Fred is entirely too respectful of Father's dignity."

*   *   *

The town was eerily silent as she walked along Main Street. The businesses wouldn't open for hours, and the only people she saw were a few shopkeepers stocking their windows or sweeping in front of their stores. So as Louisa climbed the steps to the jailhouse, she was surprised to hear a loud, familiar voice coming from inside.

"I didn't *want* anyone to pay the tax," Henry Thoreau said in the outraged tone of someone who has repeated the sentence many times. "I deliberately didn't pay it, and I'm more than happy to stay in jail to protest."

The sheriff looked weary. "Henry, the tax is paid. I can't keep you in jail so you can make some sort of political point. Go home." He ran his hand through his hair. "In fact, if you insist on staying, I'll have to start charging you for your room and board."

"Then tell me who paid it!" Henry said angrily. "I'll set him straight and teach him to meddle in my affairs." At that moment he noticed Louisa. She raised her eyebrows at the word "affairs," and Henry flushed crimson and began pacing about the lobby.

She took advantage of his momentary silence to ask for her father. The sheriff was courteous and led her back to the nearest cell. "He spent a comfortable night, Miss Alcott. Dr. Bartlett already looked in on him this morning and said he's fine to go home. Send for Dr. Bartlett if your father has any bad headaches."

Louisa held out her hand to thank him. "We're very grateful for you taking care of him last night. Is there any news about your investigation?"

The sheriff grimaced. "Not much. No one knows much about this fellow, so it's hard to see what might have gotten him killed. But the landlady at his boardinghouse told us he always had a thick wallet. We didn't find it on the body. So I'm inclined to think he was followed to the Emersons' . . . building? What do you call that thing?"

Louisa smiled. "Well, Mrs. Emerson calls it the Ruin."

"A good name," the sheriff said with a chuckle. "If that building lasts through next winter, I'll eat my hat." His demeanor became serious. "I suspect a thief followed Finch there. He didn't want a witness, so he knocked your father out. Maybe Finch drew his gun to defend himself and the thief shot him. We're talking to the usual suspects . . ."

"The usual suspects?" Louisa asked faintly.

"We know who the troublemakers are in town. We always pull them in if something happens. But in this case, unless we get lucky, I don't think we'll ever know who killed him."

Fortunately for George, Louisa thought.

"Here's your father," the sheriff said. The door was ajar as if to emphasize that Bronson was not a prisoner. "I'd better go back and deal with Mr. Thoreau."

As he turned to leave, Louisa touched his arm. "Sheriff, who did pay his tax? Who even knew he was in jail?"

The sheriff grinned and in a conspiratorial whisper, said, "Your friend Mr. Fred Llewellyn, that's who. As soon as he heard that Henry Thoreau was in jail, he arranged to pay his fine."

"Fred did that?" Louisa asked. "Was it a lot of money?"

"Not too much," the sheriff said. He named a figure that would have kept the Alcotts eating for several weeks. Louisa thought that Fred must have used the money he had brought to contribute to the housekeeping. He might regret his altruism when he ate his tenth consecutive meal of apples. "But he asked me under any circumstances not to tell Henry who paid his fine."

"Fred probably didn't understand Mr. Thoreau's position on the tax or Fred wouldn't have paid it," Louisa explained. "Speaking of Mr. Thoreau, does he know about Mr. Finch's death?"

The sheriff shrugged. "I doubt it. He was alone in his cell all night and spitting mad this morning as soon as I told him he was free to go."

"Thank you again, Sheriff Staples." Louisa opened the door to her father's cell.

Bronson was sitting up, his hand touching a professional-looking bandage tied around his head. "Good morning, Louisa," he said. His color was poor and Louisa agreed with the doctor that her father needed rest.

"Father, I'm here to bring you home," she said. "Can you walk?"

He got to his feet, using the wall to brace himself. Louisa took his arm and led him out of the cell.

Back in the lobby, Henry was still furious, demanding to know who had ruined his plans to stage a protest. With a wink at Louisa, the sheriff said, "Mr. Thoreau, did I say the tax was paid by a man?"

"A woman!" Henry suddenly went silent, as if he'd run out of air to complain. As surely as if he had said it aloud, Louisa could see what he was thinking. His expression registered surprise when he saw Bronson, but he had more urgent concerns.

"Father, wait here," she said quietly. "I need to have a quick word with Henry." Bronson's eyes were still glassy and he sat on a convenient bench without complaint.

Henry spoke for Louisa's ears only. "Was it Lidian?" Henry said. "She heard I needed help so she paid for me. What an angel. She couldn't know that I wanted to stay in prison."

"Henry, Finch is dead!" Louisa said, more abruptly than she'd planned, but it was the only way to break through his self-centered musings.

Henry staggered back. "Dead? How?"

"He was shot yesterday. Didn't you wonder why Father was here? And Fred?"

Henry shrugged. "I can't say I thought about it much. I've been planning an essay on civil disobedience." His blue eyes suddenly darkened with fear. "Did Lidian shoot him?"

"Lidian didn't do it," Louisa assured him quickly. "She was with me when we heard the gunshot." He exhaled his relief loudly. "But she was afraid you had."

"But I've been here, in prison."

"Lidian didn't know that," Louisa said.

"Then who paid my fine?" Henry said.

Louisa's mouth made an involuntary irritated noise. "When you are finished worrying about yourself, perhaps you should go to her. You'll relieve her mind," Louisa suggested.

"I'll go now." Henry started to leave, then thought better of it and turned back to Louisa. "You should know that I'm going to break it off between us. Finch may be dead, and heaven knows I won't mourn him, but what happened yesterday has shown me that Lidian is too vulnerable. I can't put her reputation in harm's way."

"I think that's wise," Louisa said. "Henry, before you go, can you tell me one thing?"

He nodded warily.

She pulled the wooden horse from her pocket. "Is this the horse you were carving yesterday?" she asked.

The look of relief on his face was almost comical. "How do you have it? I thought I tossed it in the woods."

"Is it the same?" she asked, her voice urgent.

He took it and examined it closely. Nodding, he said, "I remember this knot in the wood; I thought it would do for the horse's mane. But it didn't work."

"You're certain?" Louisa asked.

"Yes," he said with impatience. "Now, Louisa, I have to go to Lidian. Goodbye." He hurried out, running out without even acknowledging Bronson's weak greeting.

Louisa joined her father. His clothing was rumpled and his hair stuck up on his head like a halo. She tried to smooth it down, but he batted away her hand. "Louisa, just take me home. I want to sleep in my own bed."

"I will, Father," she said. "But I have to ask you a few questions first."

"I've answered questions until I can't stand another!" Bronson said in an irritated tone.

"But did you answer them truthfully?" Louisa retorted. He drew himself up, ready to scold her for impertinence, but she hushed him. "Father, it is demeaning to both of us if you lie to me. Why don't I tell you what I've deduced and you can tell me if I've made a mistake."

He shot her a piercing glare, his eyes suddenly clear. "Go on," he said finally.

"You were *not* alone all day," Louisa said. "Beth brought you some food, including fresh strawberries. You hurried her away so you could meet with Miss Whittaker—I'll give you the benefit of the doubt there and say the meeting was innocent. I tend to think she flattered you and appealed to your vanity. But when she came, she told you she'd made a fool of you. She's a swindler, and she was using you from the day she arrived." She glanced sidelong at her father. He stared straight ahead and didn't contradict her version of events.

"She also told you that Mr. Finch, who we knew only as a slave catcher, was also a criminal. She gave you enough information to make Sheriff Staples very interested in Finch."

Bronson stroked his chin. "She knew I would do the right thing. And it would have removed him as a threat to George." At the mention of George, his face clouded. "You haven't told the sheriff about him?"

"No," Louisa assured him. "But my story isn't finished. A little while later, Finch found you at the gazebo."

"He threatened to make Miss Whittaker's fraud public. He thought that would be so humiliating that I wouldn't report him to the sheriff." Bronson snorted. "I soon set him right. A man such as me is often misunderstood. If I were easily embarrassed, I'd have given up my ideas long ago."

Louisa glanced at him. Arrogant as he might be, he was also consistent. It was admirable in an aggravating sort of way. "I know, Father," she said softly.

"I told him as soon as my work was done, I was going to find Sheriff Staples. I turned my back on him and that was the last thing I remember."

Louisa nodded. "I thought it might be something like that. Your friend Miss Whittaker taunted Finch and your poor head took the brunt of it."

They were almost to Hillside when her father stopped short and grabbed her arm. "About George. I saw him running away. I think he saw Finch attack me and he tried to help. Who knows, perhaps Finch was going to kill me and George saved my life. He's suffered enough; we can't let him face the consequences."

Louisa reached their gate and held it open for her father. "George is gone, Father. Whatever happens to him is out of our hands."

CHAPTER
TWENTY-ONE

"You'll be sorry some day, Jo."
"Oh, where are you going?" she cried, for
his face frightened her.
"To the devil!" was the consoling answer.

Father's homecoming was all he could have wished;
Beth made such a fuss of him. Fred arranged the sofa for the
invalid and brought him pillows. Once Father was comfortably ensconced under a quilt, he demanded breakfast, because,
he told them, breakfast in the jail had been awful.

"What would you like, Father?" Beth asked.

"Perhaps an omelet?" was his answer.

Beth's face fell. Her omelets always turned out leathery. Louisa, concealing a smile, took pity on her. "I'll make you one, Father. Marmee taught me how."

A cloud passed over Father's face at the mention of Marmee. As he drifted off to sleep, he muttered, "Maybe when she hears about my injury, she'll come home."

Louisa and Beth returned to the kitchen, where Fred sat at the table, happy to watch them cook while he snacked on the last of the strawberries.

"Beth, get out the frying pan and put in a bit of fat," Louisa said. "I'll get some eggs from the henhouse. Fred, can you hand me that basket?"

Fred stared at the wall.

"Fred?" Louisa repeated.

"Oh, sorry. Here it is." He reached up and unhooked the basket from its hook. As she walked outside, Louisa wondered about Beth's basket. Why had it been taken and discarded along the path? There was no reason for it she could see.

She pushed open the door and immediately a swarm of chickens surrounded her feet, looking for feed. She gently shoved them out of her way with the toe of her boot and went to the shelves where they laid their eggs. She'd collected a dozen or so when she noticed a dark shape in the corner. She peered into the shadows and then recoiled. It was a man crouched on the ground.

"George?" Louisa gasped. She held up the basket to ward him off, then realized how foolish that was. If George were going to hurt her, a basket full of eggs would not deter him.

George straightened up but kept his distance. "Miss Alcott, I didn't kill him. I swear to God."

Her hand on the door handle behind her back, Louisa considered this. "If you didn't kill him, why did you run?" she asked.

"I ran back here!" he cried.

Puzzled, Louisa decided to start with the basics. "Why were you even at the gazebo?"

"Your father asked me to bring him those crooked branches. When I got there, Mr. Alcott was lying on the ground and the slave catcher was dead. I was about to help your father when he woke up." George covered his face with his large hands. In the dim light, it was as though he had disappeared, and when he spoke his voice was disembodied. "I'm ashamed to say so, but I was afraid. So I ran."

Louisa quickly ran down the events in her mind. Everything he said fit. Except for one thing. "But George, why didn't you stay in the barn?"

"Fred told me that if they found me then I'd be hanged for sure. No one would believe an escaped slave's story. He told me if I wanted to see my family again, I had to run. So I did. But then last night, while I was sleeping rough in the woods, I did some hard thinking. I didn't kill that man, and I knew that you and Mr. Alcott would hear me out."

"Fred told you to run?" Louisa repeated in a faint voice.

In the dark, she felt rather than saw him nod. "Yes, ma'am. He's a kind and generous man. He gave me money. A lot of it."

In Louisa's mind it was as if all the details of the murder, all the clues, every conversation were dropped into a kaleidoscope and then turned, making a new pattern. All of Louisa's assumptions shifted. Her hand went to the wooden horse in her pocket. A Trojan horse, she thought. But instead of causing havoc, this horse would contribute to justice.

"George," she said. "Do you still have the handkerchief that Beth gave you?"

He pulled it from his pocket; she could see the square of white. "Of course."

"George," she said finally. "I want you to go back to the barn. Beth will bring you some food. Finch is dead; no one else is looking for you."

Ducking his head, he asked, "What about my family?"

"The Conductor says your family will be here tomorrow night."

"So soon?" The hope in his voice made her heart twist in her chest.

"Yes. So go now, before there's much traffic on the road." She turned and went back to the kitchen. Beth was alone, setting the table. Handing the basket of eggs to Beth, Louisa sat at the table, her head in her hands.

"Louisa, are you ill?" Beth asked.

"Beth, how many handkerchiefs did you sew for George?" Louisa asked suddenly.

Taken aback, Beth hesitated. "Tell me," Louisa said fiercely. "It's more important than you know."

"I've fabric enough for four," Beth said. "I've finished two so far. One I gave to George, but the other I gave to . . ."

"Fred?" Louisa asked.

"How did you know? When he beat the carpets, he was perspiring and I offered him a handkerchief."

"Beth, I'm going outside. I need you to do one thing for me."

"Anything."

"Tell Fred that George is back."

"George came back?" Beth exclaimed. "But that's good news, isn't it? Why do you look so stricken?"

Louisa pushed herself up from the table and moved toward the door. "Just tell him." The door slammed behind her.

*   *   *

She didn't have long to wait. Before a quarter hour had passed, Fred came to her on the hill. He was carrying his suitcase.

Careful not to touch her, he sat down next to Louisa. The silence between them felt like a wall. "You know, don't you?" he asked.

She nodded.

"How?" he asked. "I told George to run, but that can't be all. There must be more."

"Much more," she said. "You were the one to discover the body. How convenient if you were the one who killed him."

"It was such a simple lie," he said. "I just left out the part where he died." He leapt up and began pacing along the narrow path. "It wasn't murder, Louisa. I swear it. It was self-defense. Or at the very least, it was defense of your father. As I was coming up to the gazebo, I heard Finch and your father arguing so I hurried to be of service to Bronson. I arrived just in time to see Finch crashing a heavy branch over his head. I was afraid he would kill Bronson. I charged at him. We fought. This time he didn't get the better of me so easily," he said. Louisa winced to hear the bravado in his voice.

"He pulled out that damned gun. I struggled with him, trying to get it away from him. It went off." He knelt in front of her and buried his face in the fabric of her skirt. "He was dead. It was an accident. You must believe me."

Louisa hesitated, then touched his tousled hair. "I do," she said softly. "But what happened next isn't so easily explained."

"Your father was still unconscious but breathing. I knew you wouldn't be far behind me. My only thought was to get rid of the gun and any evidence that I had fired it. I wiped my hands as clean as I could and wrapped the gun in a hand-kerchief. But then I saw Beth's basket. I couldn't let her be involved. She might be questioned, and she's far too fragile for that. So I took it with me." He twisted his body so that he was still on the ground but next to Louisa's legs. He rested his head against her knee.

"Where were you going?" she asked, her voice low and calm so he would keep talking.

"I couldn't take the path that led back to you, so I left by the path that leads here. I needed a place to hide the gun. When I remembered the post office, I decided it would do for a temporary spot. I ran like the dickens. The rain started and I was grateful because it took off all the gunpowder from my skin, but it made the path even more treacherous."

"You were out of breath," Louisa said, remembering. "But I didn't think anything of it."

"When I was almost at Hillside I realized that I couldn't keep Beth's basket. How could I explain why I had it? I couldn't afford to have anyone guess that I had come back to Hillside. So I tossed it in the underbrush. I was shocked when I saw it in the kitchen."

"Why did you leave the gun in the post office?" Louisa asked. "When I found it I immediately questioned the story that George was guilty. He couldn't have known about our secret spot. And if he was going to run, wouldn't he keep the gun?"

His admiring smile was a pale imitation of what it had been a few days earlier. "I tried to retrieve it last night, but you insisted that I come inside with you. And I didn't dare sneak out later; you so easily hear me from your room." He sighed. "I should have done it anyway." He got to his feet and faced her. "What made you first suspect me?"

Louisa pulled the wooden horse out of her pocket. "I found this at the clearing. But Henry carved it only that morning. No one could have taken it except him or you. And he was in jail." She turned the horse over in her hands. "At first I thought it was left there deliberately to cast suspicion on Henry. That's why I took it away. But once I discovered that Henry had been in jail the entire time, I thought it must have been left accidentally."

Fred's grin was twisted. "I wanted a memento of him to take back to school with me. It must have fallen out of my pocket in the struggle. I didn't even know I had lost it." He placed his palm against his forehead as though he was trying to remember.

"And then there was the money," Louisa said. "Why did you take it?"

"To make it seem to be a robbery," Fred said. "And it worked, didn't it?"

"Until you paid Henry's fine. That made me wonder how a poor man could do that. But when George told me that you gave him a lot of money, I realized where the money had come from."

"I'm sure it's not a consolation," Fred said, "but I also paid Dr. Bartlett, the general store, and the stationer. You can hold your head up high in Concord now."

Louisa held herself very still for a moment, collecting herself. She slowly got to her feet. "Don't make me complicit in your crimes. I'm poor, yes, and I hate it. But I've never stolen a penny. Nor would I let my debts be paid with stolen money. That you would think I would that tells me everything about your character." Her voice dropped to a husky whisper. "And how little you know about mine."

"I've not been a saint, but not a complete sinner, either. I should have told you everything, but I was afraid." Fred balled his fists up as though he was trying to keep hold of something that was slipping away from him. "Can't you forgive me?"

"Aren't you forgetting the worst thing? The thing I find most inexcusable?"

Not meeting her eyes, he scuffed the dirt with the toe of his boot. "What?"

"You tried to fix the blame on George."

Fred replied, "I would have much preferred to use Miss Whittaker as my stalking horse, or Pryor. But you, as always, were too clever for me. You cleared her, and George was the only one left."

"While you were at it, why not blame Father? Or Henry?"

Fred looked at her with horror. "I could never do that! They're my friends, and great men."

"But George was expendable? After all, he's only a slave when all is said and done." Louisa was implacable, her jaw clenched and eyes blinking to keep from weeping.

He reached for her hand, but she pulled it away. "Louisa, it wasn't like that. George was the only suspect who you would be content to let go free. There were so many ways to rationalize George killing a man like Finch."

"And how did you rationalize it, Fred?" Louisa tasted bile in her mouth to match her bitter words. "What excellent reason did you use to justify killing a man and deliberately incriminating another?"

Fred's hand dropped. "So you can't forgive me, then?"

Her silence was his answer.

Fred turned away and gazed down at Hillside. To Louisa his tragic posture was that of an exile looking upon his home, knowing it was lost to him forever. "What are you going to do?" he asked.

"Right now, I'm going back to the house to make my father an omelet. I'll tell him everything and we'll decide what to do together. But I doubt he'll want to turn you in. He thinks of you as a son. He likes you better than me, if truth be told."

"Louisa . . ."

With a quick but definite shake of her head, she silenced him. "Whatever we choose to do, it will take a day or two before the sheriff is involved. An enterprising young man can go anywhere in that time."

"So that's it?" he asked. "Just like that, our history and our future wiped out?" His voice was rough and without looking at him, she knew he was crying.

"I would have stood by you if the killing was all there was. Even the robbery. But what you tried to do to George was cowardly and unforgivable. I thought better of you." She walked past him without looking back. Only when she got to the kitchen door did she glance up the hill to where he had been.

Fred was gone. But Beth and her father were waiting for their breakfast.

EPILOGUE
THREE MONTHS LATER

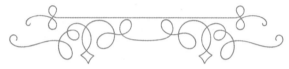

"Jo, don't get despondent or do rash things,
write to me often,
and be my brave girl, ready to help and cheer all."

*D*earest Marmee,

I can't tell you how overjoyed we all are that you are coming home! We have missed you terribly. Beth is beside herself with happiness and Father did a little jig in the parlor when he thought no one was watching.

I want to make sure this letter makes the evening post, so I'll be brief and just tell you the news so that when you return we can concentrate on celebrating.

We have heard good news from our "package." He and his own packages made it to Canada safely. I'm so proud that we helped in a such noble cause. There have been no more packages, but that may be because Mr. Pryor has retired. He decided he had too many secrets to be useful anymore.

Mr. Emerson decided not to charge Miss Whittaker. He said it is enough that she will never darken his door again. He is going on a lecture tour for several months out West. This time, though, he didn't ask Henry to stay at the house. Henry is busy writing, and I think staying at the Emerson house would only be a distraction. Lidian Emerson is quite capable of looking after herself and the children. (They've come back from Boston with new clothes and fancy airs—but Ellen is once again my student and the barn is being used as a school again.)

I told you how Fred left school and joined a merchant ship. I doubt he will return to Concord again.

You told me to write every day, and I have. Father and I are getting much better now that I am pouring all my bad temper onto the page. I've a story I want to show you when you come home. Before you say anything, Marmee dear, let me tell you that these tales of blood, thunder, and romance will never be published. Or if they are, not under my own name. But they do seem to suit my temperament more than sweet stories with morals and heroines who are too good to be true!

Travel safely.

Love,

Louisa

AUTHOR'S NOTE

At the time of her death at age fifty-five, Louisa May Alcott was a wealthy woman. She supported her parents, Abba ("Marmee") and Bronson, and her three sisters. After decades of poverty, Louisa ensured that her parents' last years were comfortable and debt-free. She had earned every cent with her pen and wrote more than thirty books.

Louisa began writing in her teens, frequently entering what she called her creative "vortex." She wrote so furiously that she trained herself to be ambidextrous; when one hand tired, she switched her pen to the other. Her first (unpublished) novel was called *The Inheritance*. There is no record about when Louisa wrote the novel, but we know it was finished by the time she was seventeen. So I took the liberty of having her write it during this story and describing the plot to Fred. It was only rediscovered in 1988.

Unusually for the time, Louisa was able to earn a living writing gothic romances and horror stories. Since these stories were not considered ladylike, she wrote under an assumed name, A. M. Barnard. Even today, scholars are discovering new stories by A. M. Barnard, also known as Louisa May Alcott. She made a good living, but her earnings in her early years of writing were never quite enough to support her entire family and pay off the debts they owed.

During the Civil War, Louisa was determined to help the Union cause. She went to Washington, D.C., to work as a nurse in a hospital. She wrote home about the terrible conditions she saw there as well as the bravery of the injured troops. Later she turned her letters into *Hospital Sketches*, a slightly fictionalized account of a nurse's experience in a military hospital. It was published under her own name to great acclaim.

Louisa's writing was not her only souvenir from her war service. She contracted typhoid and was dosed with a medicine containing mercury. She suffered ill health for the rest of her life, possibly from heavy metals poisoning.

In Louisa's mid-thirties, after she had had moderate success as a writer, her publisher approached her with a proposition: to write books for young girls. Louisa was hesitant. She preferred her "blood and thunder" stories. The publisher was insistent and finally she agreed. But the only stories for girls she could think of were her own experiences at Hillside as a teenager. With the wholehearted support of her family, she began writing scenes from her childhood.

For those readers who have not yet had the pleasure of reading *Little Women,* there are four fictional March sisters, each distinct from the other but charming in their own way, just as in the Alcott family. The main character, Jo March, is a tomboy with literary aspirations. Louisa modeled Jo upon herself and the other girls on her own sisters.

Louisa thought her first pages were quite dull, but to appease her publisher, she sent them anyway. He agreed they were dull. But happily, he gave her story to his young niece, who couldn't get enough of the March sisters. He decided to publish the book.

Little Women was a huge sensation, much to Louisa's surprise. The novel was so successful that her public immediately clamored for a sequel. For the rest of her life, Louisa had only to write about the March sisters to have an instant bestseller. While the money was gratifying, Louisa admitted that she would have preferred to have written novels with more adult themes.

Little Women reads like a biography of the Alcott family. In fact, if you visit the Alcott house today, the docents will use the names of the Alcott girls and their March counterparts interchangeably.

Louisa's sisters' fortunes were echoed in the novels. Anne, her older sister, is Meg in the stories. Like Meg, Anne married a local man and had two sons. When Anne's husband died, Louisa wrote *Jo's Boys* and assigned the royalties to her nephews.

May is Amy in the novel, and like Amy, she was an artist. Louisa paid for May to go to Paris, where she became a successful painter. May married a count and had a baby girl, Lulu. Sadly, May died a few weeks later. Louisa raised the little girl.

Sickly Lizzie's counterpart was Beth, and alas, like Beth she died young, probably having contracted scarlet fever from one of her mother's charity cases.

Louisa's relationship with her father is central to understanding her character. Louisa admired her father but resented that his principles seemed to preclude him from earning a living. Bronson Alcott preferred to think and write rather than work, subjecting his large family to poverty that at times grew desperate. Based on her personal experience, Louisa once described a philosopher as "A man up in a balloon with his family at the strings tugging to pull him down."

Of all the members of Louisa's family, her father is conspicuously absent from most of *Little Women*, perhaps her way of expressing her disappointment in him. Ironically, after the publication of *Little Women*, Bronson made a fortune lecturing about his life as the father of the *Little Women*.

Bronson Alcott was one of the Transcendentalist philosophers. They believed in the inherent goodness of people and importance of nature. Stressing self-reliance and independence, Transcendentalism is considered one of the first American intellectual movements. Ralph Waldo Emerson and Henry David Thoreau were considered leaders of the movement.

Abba "Marmee" Alcott came from a wealthy pedigreed family. They considered that she had married far beneath her when she married a poor farmer's son who hadn't even had a formal education. Certainly her pampered upbringing had not prepared her for life with Bronson.

Over the course of their marriage, the Alcotts moved twenty-nine times, always looking for less expensive lodging.

At first Abba's family helped generously, but eventually they grew frustrated that Bronson could not support the family. However, their elegant houses in Boston often hosted the Alcott girls, exposing Louisa to a style of life she always envied.

Louisa was very close to her mother, Marmee. Marmee gave her her first pen, encouraging her to write as a safety valve for her strong emotions that might otherwise overwhelm her. Louisa was the daughter most like her mother, and Marmee got into the habit of confiding her troubles to Louisa, including their financial struggles.

At the urging of Bronson's friend and mentor, Ralph Waldo Emerson, the family settled in Concord in 1844. Bronson briefly relocated the family to Fruitlands, his utopian community. Fruitlands was a colossal failure, lasting only seven months, and it nearly broke up the Alcott family. Afterwards a humiliated Bronson went through a long period of depression. He only recovered when they returned to Concord and bought Hillside with a small inheritance from Abba's father. Marmee decided that if Bronson was not able to support them, she would. In 1846, at the start of this story, Abba left her family and went to work in New Hampshire.

At Hillside, the family knew several years of stability, if not prosperity. Louisa was particularly happy to have a room of her own. Bronson proved to be a good farmer and a clever carpenter. They lived simply, eating a vegetarian diet; Bronson was against using animals against their will, so they ate no meat and used no leather. He would have preferred that the family not wear wool, but Abba insisted. For a time the family also didn't wear cotton, to protest the use of slaves in cotton picking.

Ralph Waldo Emerson lived a few minutes down the road and Louisa was a frequent visitor. She was one of the few people Emerson allowed into his library. As an adult, Louisa confessed her childhood crush on Emerson.

Emerson was hugely respected in town, although many people raised their eyebrows at his friendship with and support of the Alcotts, who were considered very odd by the townspeople. One local wit said that "Emerson was a seer and Alcott was a seersucker." One way that Bronson tried to repay his friend was by building Emerson a gazebo. The structure was so unusual that people in town mocked it and Mrs. Emerson called it a "Ruin." Bronson had the last laugh, however, when the gazebo lasted almost twenty years.

The family's other great friend was Henry David Thoreau. He had a reputation for being surly, but children adored him. He led them on trips into the woods to explore. Louisa and her friends recalled many boating trips with Thoreau on Walden Pond. He would play his flute, literally charming birds out of the trees.

Thoreau was a great friend of Emerson's, working as his handyman and even moving into the house when Emerson traveled to Europe. Emerson's wife, Lidian, was an attractive woman and Thoreau admired her greatly. They met for the first time when Thoreau spied her through a window and threw her a poem attached to a small bouquet of flowers. There is no evidence that their relationship was ever anything more than friendship, although some biographers have speculated that it was.

Henry's cabin at Walden Pond is justly famous as the subject of *Walden*, his reflections about living simply. He wanted to live away from society and learn what nature had to teach him. Bronson helped him build the cabin on Emerson's land. Louisa and her friends were frequent visitors. Its remote location made it the perfect place for a fictional assignation and possibly a hiding place for a fugitive slave.

Thoreau was arrested for nonpayment of taxes by the sheriff and tax collector Sam Staples and spent one night in jail before his tax was paid by an unknown person. He wrote about this night in his essay "Civil Disobedience." This event took place several months after my story, but I could not resist including it—what better alibi for Henry David Thoreau than his infamous night in jail?

Fred Llewellyn was based on a composite of two people in Louisa's life. She had a distant cousin who came to stay with them. He and Louisa were companions and he described her at the most beautiful runner he had ever seen. He adored the entire family and even wrote a memoir about them. He grew up to be a respected doctor and a lifelong friend of Louisa's. As an adult, Louisa recalled another boy, unnamed, who went away to school and came back "so big and handsome . . . I could not recover myself for several minutes. Blushingly I

agreed to go boating and berrying and all the rest of it again."
She goes on to say she never went and a few weeks later he
died of fever and Louisa never saw him again. Combining
these two characters made for a fun companion for Louisa as
she solves the mystery and hints at a sad end for Fred.

The presence of a fugitive slave in Concord drives this
story. The Alcotts were vocal abolitionists, protesters against
slavery. They were active in the Underground Railroad, a
secret organization that smuggled slaves out of the South to
the Northern states or Canada. It was illegal to aid fugitive
slaves in 1846, and the Alcotts could have gone to jail.

Louisa recalled a man named George who stayed with
them for a week. The work of the Railroad was shrouded in
secrecy, so we don't know where the Alcotts would have
hidden him. Since the barn dated back to the American
Revolution, I took the liberty of adding a secret room where
George can hide.

Where there are fugitive slaves, there are mysteries and
secrets and, best of all, sinister slave catchers. The reward for
an educated slave could easily be $1,000 (in today's currency
that would be $30,000). Aside from his name, in this story
George is as fictional as Finch, the man chasing him.

Finally, the character of Miss Whittaker was based on
stories of young women who flocked to the Transcendentalist
philosophers to listen eagerly to their pronouncements. After
my story takes place, one such woman, very attractive and
well-to-do, appeared in Bronson's life, no doubt giving Abba a

few worrisome moments. Miss Whittaker is my invention, and as far as I know, Emerson, Alcott, and Thoreau were never victimized by a confidence scheme.

Louisa died at the age of fifty-six from a stroke, outliving her younger sisters and her mother. She never married. She did get to travel to Europe several times, fulfilling a lifelong dream.

Little Women is still one of the most beloved books in American literature. How surprised Louisa would be to learn that her sketches about her childhood still resonate with so many readers nearly 150 years later. Louisa gave Jo March, her fictional counterpart, this line, which proved to be prophetic: "I think I shall write books, and get rich and famous, that would suit me, so that is my favorite dream."

FURTHER READING

*T*o learn about Louisa's life, you should read *Little Women*. Her posthumously published first novel, *The Inheritance*, is also readily available. And do yourself a favor and read her thrillers, collected in *Behind a Mask: The Unknown Thrillers of Louisa May Alcott* and *A Marble Woman: The Unknown Thrillers of Louisa May Alcott*.

There are several excellent biographies of Louisa that I would recommend.

Susan Cheever's biography, *Louisa May Alcott: A Personal Biography* (Simon and Schuster, 2010), is a breezy examination of Louisa's life from the perspective of the child of a famous writer. Eve LaPlante is a member of the Alcott family and considers Louisa's relationship with Marmee in *Marmee and Louisa: The Untold Story of Louisa May Alcott and Her Mother* (Free Press, 2012). John Matteson won the Pulitzer Prize for biography for *Eden's Outcasts: The Story of Louisa May Alcott and Her Father* (W. W. Norton and Co, 1997), which focuses on Louisa's father.

Two other biographies that I found very useful were Harriet Reisen's *Louisa May Alcott: The Woman Behind Little Women* (Picador, 2009) and Madeleine B. Stern's Louisa May Alcott (Northeastern, 1950).

In 2009, the PBS series American Masters screened a documentary called *Louisa May Alcott: The Woman Behind Little Women*. Portions of it are available online. It's wonderful!

If you have the opportunity, you can tour Louisa May Alcott's home in Concord, Massachusetts. The house is called Orchard House and it is next door to Hillside. The Alcotts left Hillside to move to Boston. Several years later they returned to Concord and bought Orchard House, which is now the Louisa May Alcott museum. Many of the scenes in *Little Women* are set in Orchard House. Ralph Waldo Emerson's nearby house is also a museum.

ACKNOWLEDGMENTS

I love writing about fascinating young women, perhaps because I have two "little women" of my own. Rowan and Margaux are a constant inspiration.

Tanya Lee Stone gave me the benefit of her insights into the historical lives of interesting women. Patricia Reilly Giff shared her library and offered generous support of my interpretation of Louisa May Alcott.

My critique group is my rock, always. Sari Bodi, Christine Pakkala, and Karen Swanson—many thanks for your tough critiques.

The Chronicle team is always wonderful. Thank you to my editor, Victoria Rock, who has the knack of asking the right questions. Taylor Norman is always helpful both on the editing and technical sides. Sara Schneider designed the book and the exciting cover. Lara Starr, Stephanie Wong, and Jaime Wong are my go-to ladies for help with publicity and marketing.

The staff at the Orchard House and the Ralph Waldo Emerson house were very helpful and knowledgeable. Most are volunteers and writers like me would be lost without them.

Last but never least, to my husband, Rob. Our family may not be as idyllic as the Marches', but over the past thirty years we've built a life filled with love and laughter. I write because you make it possible.